Deitch's PICTORAMA

Introduction by Gene Deitch — page 2

The Sunshine Girl — page 4

THE GOLEM — page 82

Unlikely Hours — page 125

Children of Aruf — page 157

THE COP ON THE BEAT — page 167

Further Reading — page 198

Biographies — page 200

Introduction by

OK, comics are in our blood. I grew up in the golden age of the American newspaper comic strip. My parents subscribed to Hearst's *Los Angeles Examiner*. The right-wing politics meant nothing to an 8-year-old kid; what meant everything was that it had the best King Features comics, an entire page of dailies and a huge Sunday color section with the mysterious name, "Puck."

From 1932 onward, I devoured the comics, and carefully copied the characters on my drawing pads. I loved to draw, and was good at it, so naturally I dreamed of one day drawing my own comic strip. Amazingly, I eventually did it — had my own nationally syndicated comic strip, which you may well have never heard of, "Terr'ble Thompson." It ran less than a year, because another dream — animation — overtook it. But now look right here: something I never dreamed of — all three of my sons are in this great Comic Pictorama book! Who could dream more than having three genius fantasy creators as sons?

I wish I could take credit for their achievements, but the fact is they did it on their own, growing to maturity during years I was working abroad. Needless to say, my parental pride runneth over. We have of course always been in touch, and as I'm only 19 years older than Kim, my oldest, I do feel I'm one of the gang, however passé I might be. I can tell you one thing: Whatever any of you parents might think, as we did at the time, that we were not going to let any so-called generation gap distance ourselves from our kids — that we were modern, progressive parents, keeping up with the talk and the ideas of the time, and would not be so retro as to be out of what's happening…

Gene Deitch

Well, the fact is that it's nearly impossible. The generation gap exists. I have to admit that while I'm working on my own cartoons I'm listening constantly to internet radio playing the swing music of the 1930s, '40s, and '50s. No matter how much I've tried to keep up, I simply can't get with anything later than The Beatles, but even they don't grab me like the basic blues of Basie. I can't stand the three-word lyrics and mindless pounding of hard rock, nor the frightening ramblings of Rap. My great luck is that even though the swing era is what I, not my sons, grew up with, it turns out that the music and culture of the era of my boyhood has somehow grabbed them, even though it was not their era. Music is one of the things that binds us together!

We have a lot to talk about with each other. We're steadily in touch in this digital era, and their creations talk to me loud and clear. We are in fact not the usual totally distanced father and sons. We share many values, ideas, and interests.

That is my great joy. We are all lovers of stories and fantasy, dinosaurs and legends, the weird and the wonderful, the bizarre and eccentric characters and parallel worlds that reflect what this desperately misshapen world we live in might rather be.

This book sums it all up. Here is a great sample of the thinking and amazing creativity of Kim, Simon, and Seth Deitch. How glad I am that not one of them saw fit to change his family name!

— Gene Deitch
Prague, November 2007

The Sunshine Girl

BY
ELEANOR
WHALEY
as told to
and
illustrated by
Kim Deitch

Introduction by Kim Deitch

January, 2007.

The former Eleanor Whaley told me this story in extensive interviews, taped over the last year and a half, on the sole condition that I tell it in her own words exactly as she told it to me. And that, outside of some perfunctory editing, is exactly what I have done.

She is twenty-six years old and lives in her own home somewhere in upstate New York. Though married, she is using her maiden name here as she does not want to draw undue attention to herself or her husband, who is currently serving with our Army in Iraq.

Kim

But life is anything but lonely for Ellie these days, for living with her, as her wards, are her uncle Garwood, his forty-six-year-old pet macaw Noodles, and her brother Sidney.

Ellie

Sidney, twenty-five, is the reigning crown bottle cap king of North America, South America, Europe and two thirds of Asia. This does not include screw-on caps and while it does include beer caps, does not include beer cans or bottles.

Sid

To me, the funny part of all this is that the answer to everything was right under our noses the whole time, so I don't want to go spinning it out like some tired old mystery story.

When Sid and me sneaked off to the city that day I remember taking a good long look at that old wrecked ship they called the Buccaneer out on the Hudson River maybe about

half a mile out, anchored so long ago, no one seemed to know where it came from or what its real name was; just that it was older than sin and us kids better stay away from it.

But even then I couldn't help thinking it had something to do with Uncle Gar and it sure as Satan did as you'll soon find out.

Like I said before, I'm not trying to make a big mystery out of this; no more than it actually was, anyway.

So, like I started to say, that day, fifteen years ago, Sid and me got on a train in our town in Westchester New York, Hastings on Hudson and were heading for New York City. Well, sneaking in, as it was Friday and we sure were skipping School. Not that that was so unusual. We did that often enough, I'm sorry to say; sneaking around alleys in town, behind restaurants, rooting

Any luck?

Naw, just a bunch of Coke screw- ons!

through garbage cans, looking; always looking for the good ones.

GOOD ONES

Good whats, you may ask. Well, it was bottle caps, pure and simple; that little piece of metal printed with colored paint that some machine stamped on a bottle leaving a crinkled edge all around; the edge that collectors call the crown.

We'd read all about it in "Crown Cap Round-up" which was the name of these small magazines we found one day in a box in our basement.

Late 1980's

Sid still had most of them stashed away except for the one Pop caught him with and tore up right before our eyes. It was the one that had a picture of the Sunshine Girl right on the cover. That was tough to take.

And hard to figure out too at first. When Sid tried to ask him about it, Pop hit Sid so hard he drew blood so we knew it was another one of those things it was best not to ask Pop about. And it probably meant that it had something to do with our Uncle Gar.

See, Pop and Gar were the best of friends growing up. Gar was older and Pop kind of looked up to him. That's what Mom told us when she was still around. She also told us Pop was never really the same after Gar died, or so everyone supposed, which wasn't really true of course, but I'll get to that.

Well, we were pretty young in 1992 to be going to the city like that all by ourselves. Sid was thirteen and I was eleven. But I was pretty grown up mentally even then. And anyway there wasn't much to it. See, it turned out the place where the crown cap convention was being held,

Copied from a family photo. KD

Gar and Ed Whaley in 1974 behind Ernie's Deli, a hot spot for "good ones."

just that one day was right across the street from Grand Central Station. All we had to do was leave out of the right end of the station, which I figured out pretty quick, and we were just about there.

It was in a building that used to be a big camera store. I guess they were still moving out 'cause there was still lots of camera stuff all over, which wasn't the problem you might have thought as there was darn little crown cap convention to see.

I guessed the folks putting it on must have been pretty disappointed since there was a lot more room than there was dealers or people to be dealt to. It was nothing like the crown cap conventions

I saw in later years; or the massive ones they have now that Sid is always trying to tell me about. Really, I doubt there were more than five dealers all told.

There were things to see, sure enough. What caught the eye right away were these huge things made of crown caps, or covered with

them, anyway. They were made by some kid from
Ohio who was there with his Mother but outside
of taking up a lot of room and as Sid pointed
out, using some rather rare crown caps here
and there, they weren't too hot. I guess the
best of them was one of those old, double winged
airplanes you see in some war movies. Judging from
the size of it, I'd almost have believed he had

the real airplane underneath all those caps. He had another one called Godzilla and, trust me, it didn't look a bit like him. And another one called the White House made all mostly of white caps that he was still working on, or in I should say.

You could go right inside and see him still working on a crown cap portrait of President Clinton.

Hello there.

Come in and see The White House, a work in progress. PLEASE remove your shoes before entering The White House.

Welcome to my White House!

But outside of Clinton's weasel grin,
it could have been anyone; no art at all
in it. And even worse, he was using his
Mother's seemingly unlimited purse to
make a circle around Clinton with full
color Miller High Life, girl-in-the-moon caps
he was buying from a beer cap
dealer who was there.
When those ran out, I looked
and saw this same kid about
to come to blows
with Sid, who'd
been watching his
buying antics with
growing fury 'til
finally there
was this kid
trying to buy a
beat up Sunshine
Soda cap off this
odd looking dealer
we'd seen coming in,
who didn't have a
table.
  Sunshine Soda!

Can you imagine? Well, it wasn't in very good condition, but Me and Sid never saw one before, you can bet your life on that.

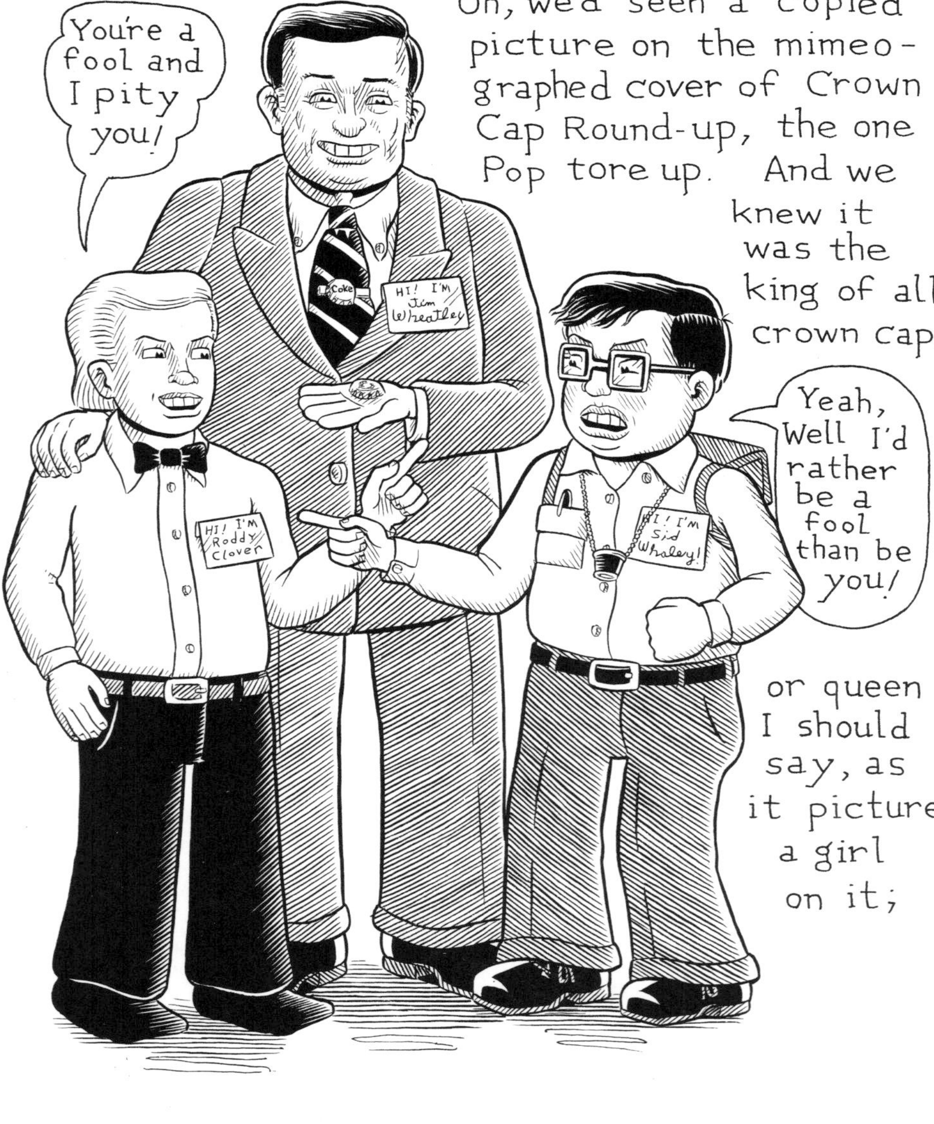
You're a fool and I pity you!
Coke
HI! I'M Jim Wheatley
HI! I'M Roddy Clover
I! I'M Sid Whaley!
Yeah, Well I'd rather be a fool than be you!

Oh, we'd seen a copied picture on the mimeo-graphed cover of Crown Cap Round-up, the one Pop tore up. And we knew it was the king of all crown caps;

or queen I should say, as it pictures a girl on it;

the Sunshine Girl, to be exact.
But I guess I don't have to tell you about it, Kim, since you drew it.* I guess you wish you had one now too, but I won't rub it in. Some day I hope you will come to appreciate, as I do, that it didn't bring any good, any real good to those that it did enrich.

Anyway, I was just about to rush in and try to break up the fight that I judged to be just seconds away from happening, when I felt a pulling at the back of my vest. Well, the person doing the pulling turned out to be a woman collector named Mildred Getz, the only woman collector there, outside of the kid

* Note: Ellie is referring here to the fact that in 1969 Aaron Garnett, a wealthy crown cap collector, hired me to design a crown cap and lease the rights to my comic strip character, Sunshine Girl, for his ill-fated Sunshine Soda.

KD

sculptor's well-heeled Mother, that is.
I soon learned that Mildred wasn't really a collector, and later, we actually did become dear friends, but just then she had this to say.

Ha! That's one cap they'll never get. Why, Jim Wheatley'd sooner sell his soul than sell that cap at any price!

Jim Wheatley!

It must have been true,

because the woman was waving five crisp, new one hundred dollar bills right under Jim Wheatley's nose! Five hundred dollars spot cash, condition be damned, for the Sunshine Girl bottle cap!

Well, of course he didn't sell it and hindsight being twenty twenty and

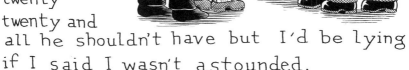

all he shouldn't have but I'd be lying if I said I wasn't astounded.

It wasn't just the big cash offer. It was the way everything was suddenly happening. If my initial reaction to the tatty con had been disappointment, well, I sure wasn't disappointed now. In seconds I had actually seen the Sunshine Girl bottle cap; the fabulous holy grail of all bottle caps.

And right before my eyes, refusing to sell it for cold cash, was none other than Jim Wheatley, editor in chief of the Crown Cap Round-up. Now I knew why he didn't have a table. It was Jim Wheatley's con! the first ever crown cap convention.

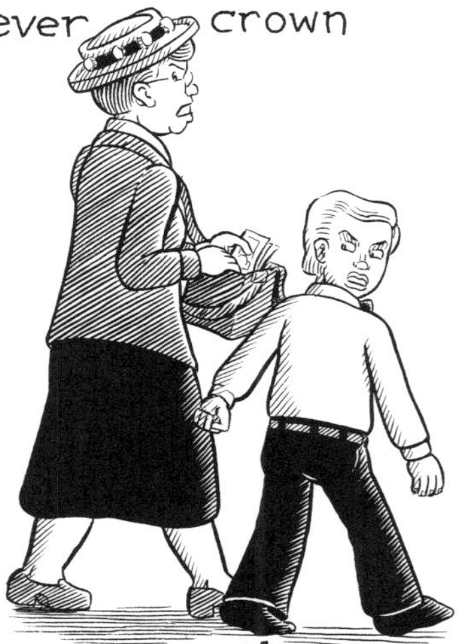

Jim was going to be the keynote speaker too, although Mildred Getz was this year's official guest of honor.

Jim had actually paid Mildred's way to the con and put her up at the Manhattan Central Hotel, which sounded a lot better than it was, as we later found out.

By the time I got over to where

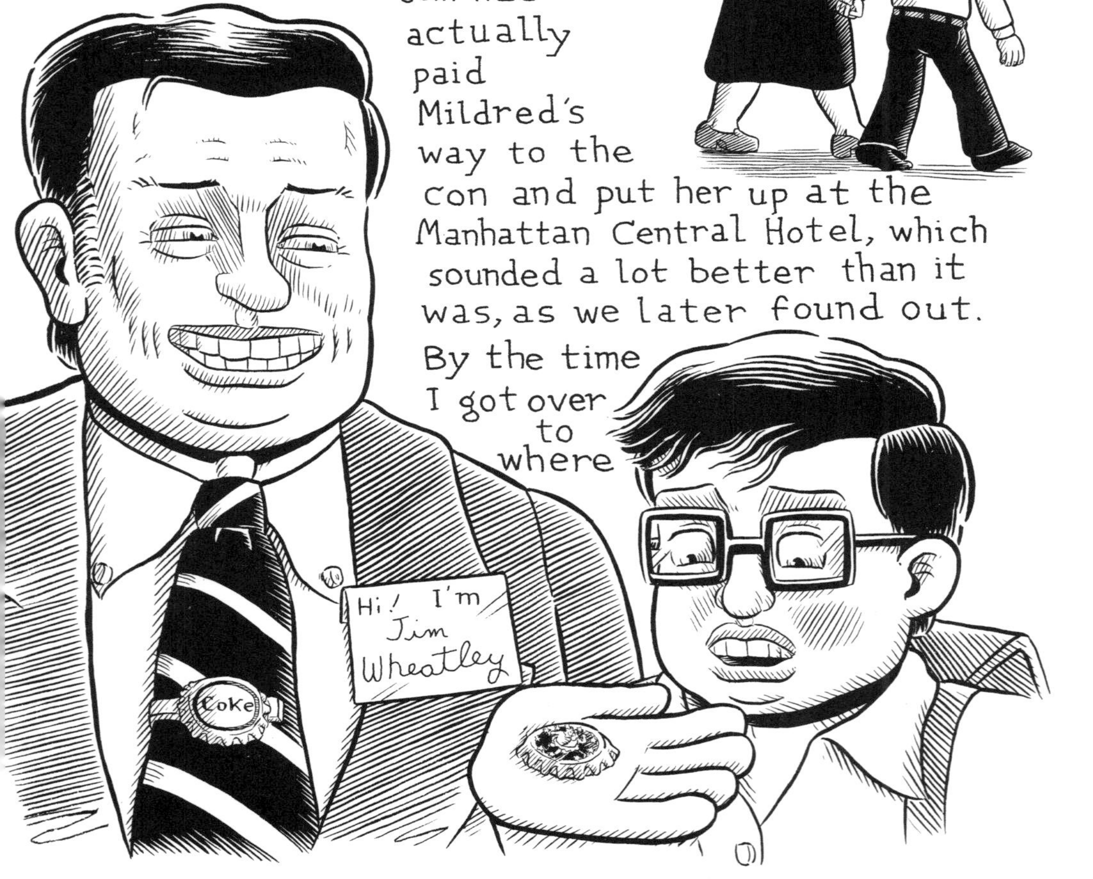
Hi! I'm Jim Wheatley
Coke

the big fight seemed about to break out, things had already simmered down. The boy sculptor and Mom Moneybags were stomping away as Mom stuffed the five hundreds back in her bottomless purse.

By now Sid and Jim were acquainted and it was Sid who actually introduced me to Jim!

Poor old Jim,

God rest his soul. Trouble was, he just wasn't much good.

but I do often pray for him.

He told us he'd already figured out who we were; told us it was written all over our faces, by which he meant we had to be kin of Gar and Ed Whaley because the family resemblance stuck out so much.

You see, Ed Whaley (our Dad) and Uncle Gar, along with Jim Wheatley, were among the true pioneers of the crown cap hobby. As boys they corresponded and when Jim first started publishing and printing Crown Cap Round-up on an old mimeograph machine, our Dad and Uncle Gar were among the first outside contributors.

Jim cranks out Round-ups on an old mimeograph in the 70's.

Of course me and Sid already knew that, having read and re-read that stash of old back issues we'd found in the basement. And later we'd managed to get new issues, ones that came out after 1976 which, of course, is how we heard about the con coming up in the city that we were now at.

Well, Mildred Getz may have been the official guest of honor, but after introductions had been made, Sid and me were pretty much getting the royal treatment as well.

"I was hoping you two would come," Jim told us, and he asked how our Dad was.

I told Jim Dad was now an officer with the Tarrytown Police in Westchester and didn't much want to know about or have anything whatsoever to do with bottle caps or collecting, which sure was true. In fact in those pre A-A days, Pop drank all his beer out of pop top cans.

Of course I didn't tell Jim that last part; only that Pop would skin us alive if he had any idea where we were today.

Jim nodded his head sadly at that in

complete understanding because he knew quite as well as we did why Daddy hated the hobby. The fact that he always sent us our copies of the round-up in a plain envelope with just a post office box for return address always seemed a pretty big hint of that to me.

See, Jim knew all about Uncle Gar or at least as much as anyone knew then.

He knew full well that Uncle Gar disappeared and probably drowned in 1976 while rooting around the ruins of an old abandoned bottling plant in Tarrytown, New York right along the edge of the Hudson River and just a few towns up from where we lived in Hastings.

HASTINGS NEWS 25¢

July 19 1976

Hope Fading For Missing Youth. Drowning Death Likely.

Mayor Suggests School Board Boondoggle.

Garwood Whaley Missing Since May

Hastings High Shuts Out Dobbs Ferry 6-2

Jim knew as well as we did that he was rooting through the ruins of the burnt out plant where in 1971 occurred a seminal moment in the history of the hobby; the raid on Aaron Garnett's Sunshine soda operation.

And, of course, me and Sid were in a better position to know about that or its aftermath because Pop never really got over that one. He did have a picture of him and Gar together hanging in the living room but he never spoke of him.

He'd gone and joined the Tarrytown Police department and I wondered about it too; if maybe that wasn't some way of trying to be in a place where he might find out more about what happened to Gar. And he got married and had Sid and me. But that same exploding temper, that we lived in fear of, finally blew his marraige apart.

We still saw Mom pretty often. She

hadn't re-married and I think she still loved Pop but just couldn't live under the same roof with him any more.

Well, getting back to Aaron Garnett. That is one thing we did learn more about that afternoon.

Jim Wheatley's slide show presentation was essentially on the lost treasures of the Aaron Garnett Collection

along with the basic facts about Aaron Garnett, the true founding father of the crown cap collecting hobby as we know it today.

So just who was Aaron Garnett? Well, he was born in 1940 and came from fairly well to do people. Nothing like the silver spooned cap sculptor and his Lady Bountiful Mom at the con, but then you didn't need quite so much money to get a good collection together in those early days.

1904 stations of the cross bottled holy water

Meet Guest of Honor MILDRED GETZ!

6th stage A woman, Veronica, wipes Jesus' face.

Jim's other cap from the set, 2nd stage, Bearing the Cross.

Jim Wheatley presents Lost Treasures of The Aaron Garnett Collection

Who was Aaron Garnett and where is he

Crown Cap Man of MYSTERY

Aaron Garnett 1940-?

Aaron Garnett even had two of the famous holy water caps. There were fourteen in all for each of the stations of the cross.*

It turned out that Mildred Getz' grand-father put these out in 1904. Coca-cola aside, they were some of the very earliest crown caps made.

Mildred's bottled, stations of the cross, Holy Water set...

in a hand made sample case made by her Grandfather August Getz.

But let's get back to Coca-cola be-cause that is where the Garnett collection really shined. Aaron Garnett had early Coke caps that nobody had, and in some cases no one, not even the Coca-cola company had any idea that they ever existed, which led to some controversy.

Note: Apparently early in the 20th century certain beverage bottle caps, along with other promotional material, were produced independently by regional distributors. KD.

In particular were his Coke movie

* a catholic meditation

series from about 1915. Aaron had four of these; Pearl White, Alice Joyce, Grace Darling and Clara Kimball Young.

There were, in fact, some accusations leveled at Aaron Garnett of forgery but they were later proven false.

It seems there's a lot we don't know about the early days of Coca-cola. I realize that a few things I'm about to say may be regarded as controversial in some quarters and quite frankly I am some-what hesitant to mention it, but think a minute.

Didn't you ever wonder about the name Coca-cola? Well, you'll never see it in the official history of Coca-cola and that's okay. It's really nothing against them but the fact is Coke came into being in the 1880's, the same time that cocaine was being developed.

Nobody actually knew just how bad cocaine really was at first; not even the father and son Doctor team that developed it and who both were turned into raging dope fiends because of it.

Hey, I'll give Coke credit where it's due. When they found out how bad cocaine actually was, they took it out and replaced it with caffeine, the same as which is in the coffee we all drink.

I wouldn't bring up any of this except that it is the thing that originally inspired Aaron Garnett and his Sunshine Soda. You see, it was that drug thing rearing its ugly head again that led to Aaron Garnett's undoing.

It was about 1965, I guess, that the whole country seemed to go drug crazy. It's a little before my time, but that's about right, isn't it, Kim? I'm guessing you ought to know. Note: Yep. KD.

Well, Aaron was about twenty-five then and like a lot of people, he got swept up into it, smoking pot, taking LSD and all manner of dope that was going around.

I guess it was Aaron's misfortune that his old father died about that time and suddenly he was a very well heeled young man and high in the new hippy social set, such as it was.

with John Lennon

with Mick Jagger and Keith Richards

Well, just like any social set, money talked and soon instead of just squandering it on rare old bottle caps, he

was also squandering it
with the hippy elite.
And he was spending
a lot of time with
that acid Guru
Timothy Leary, at
his estate in
Milbrook, New York.

Aaron and Tim Leary.

Funny! Not so far from where we are
right now; though worlds away in point of
view, for the most part.

But the thing is, even as Aaron Garnett
got higher (and more broke) there was
still one part, way in back of his drug
soaked brain, that was
still all caught up
in bottle cap glory.

And one after-
noon while
lolling around,
stoned as
usual at
Milbrook,
his big
moment of

inspiration came. And, to a large extent, it came out of all those stories that circulate about the cocaine they used to put in Coca-cola.

As Aaron saw it, cocaine in Coke was the wrong drug at the wrong time. Where as, in his mind, LSD would be the right drug at the right time.

What's more, the law was closing in on this first wave of LSD users. Tim Leary had been busted any number of times.

He was still free on bond in 1969 but it was only a matter of time before he'd be behind bars.

At Milbrook, Aaron had access to the makers of the finest, purest, *sunshine LSD being made. But its primitive distribution networks were being rapidly broken up by law enforcement.

That was when Aaron Garnett, perhaps wrong-headedly, saw his calling. Sunshine Soda, a soft drink spiked with the purest sunshine LSD, to turn on a troubled world.

You know, to tell the truth I can't help but admire the motivation. Right or wrong, the man meant well. And I can't help thinking that our Lord in Heaven maybe took that into consideration when Aaron Garnett stood in judgement before him.

*particularly good LSD in its day

See, the way I see it, there are no accidents. Everything in this world happens for a  purpose. And I'm not so sure that Aaron Garnett wasn't some kind of forerunner just like John the Baptist was the first time our Lord Jesus came.

And all these events sure did lead me to be reborn at the foot of his Holy throne.

But getting back to Aaron Garnett and trying to make a long story short. Aaron took what was left of his father's inheritance, that small part he hadn't squandered on drugs and godless bottle caps and decided to create Sunshine Soda.

Well, it got even less far than cocaine in Coke.

I got a ton of stuff on you from your old FBI file* They just figured you were too small of a fish to bother with. The fact that Garnett paid you a flat seventy-five dollars for your cap and trade mark designs was actually a blessing and you must realize that now.

Note: Actually over and above the seventy-five dollars, Aaron also gave me a rather generous supply of that good sunshine LSD. KD.

What basically happened is the police

* In 1966 many FBI files were declassified and made available to the general public through the Freedom of Information Act.

gave Aaron Garnett enough rope to hang himself with. They let him get a batch going
and then raided the secret old bottling
plant in Tarrytown, New York in 1971.

But Aaron Garnett was never found nor
was much in the way of bottling paraphernalia
ever found. A fire broke out during the raid
and the story they put out was that everything, including Aaron Garnett, probably
went up in smoke.

Of course that brings up another little
mystery. Where did Jim Wheatley get his
Sunshine Girl bottle cap?

The fact is, while I was watching Jim's
show, he was starting to seem like more
and more of a fishy character to me.

There was something else with Jim at the con that smelled funny but I'll get to that in a minute.

After the show was over Jim continued to be real nice to us. He gave us a whole mess of caps he had doubles of. In fact, he even gave Sid a slightly beat up Four color girl in the moon Miller High Life bottle cap; one that greedy kid sculptor missed out on, but that actually led to trouble.

You see, when Sid actually had that cap and I wasn't watching him he went and swapped it to the kid sculptor for one in better shape by throwing in an extra fifteen dollars on the deal.

Trouble was, that was the fifteen dollars we needed for train fare to get us back to Hastings. But you see, that's Sid all over; never thinking ahead. But again, that goes back to my idea that, really, there are no accidents, 'cause this is what happened next.

Mildred Getz happened to hear me wailing at Sid and stepped in. It turned out that she'd just about had a belly full of the con, Jim Wheatley and just about everything that went with it.

She whisked Sid and me out of there one, two, three along with all twelve of her bottled holy waters. It happened really fast because she didn't want Jim Wheatley to see her go.

Next thing you know all three of us were in a taxi heading for her room at the Manhattan Central Hotel that Jim Wheatley'd paid for. She seemed mighty relieved to be out of there too, bottles and all.

And on the cab ride over to the Manhatten Central downtown, she sure gave us an earful about what a sleazy guy Jim Wheatley was. It turned out the whole reason Jim paid Mildred's way to New York as guest of honor at the con was to try to do her out of her bottles of holy water that Mildred basically considered personal family heirlooms, having been manufactured by her Grandfather in an attempt to woo Mildred's Catholic Grandmother.

Well, August Getz got the girl, but a Papal decree engineered by a rival beer maker got the bottled holy water plan scotched dead in its tracks which accounts for why the caps are as rare as they are.

Mildred's grand parents from an old photo.

She said Jim was so desperate to get them that he was even hinting around about marriage, a prospect she found disgusting.

And, having failed at that, she suspected that he might be trying to steal them.

Now you'll never guess what happened next up in her hotel room, and it was a dump. I guess once upon a time the Manhattan Central was a fancy address but from the look of it, my guess is, it was probably some time around the civil war.

Worse yet, Jim Wheatley had the room right next to hers. There was even a connecting door from some time when the two rooms probably made up a bigger suite.

Mildred feared that Jim would try to steal the bottles and so was asking me, and not Sid (I think she had his number too.) She was asking me if I'd take the bottles and keep them for her. She told

me that looking me right in the eye saying she completely trusted me.

Well, she didn't make a mistake. I told her I'd guard them with my life and meant it too.

After that, she gave us a big feed at McDonald's, paid a cab to take us back to Grand Central and gave me money for our train ride home.

It was pretty late by the time we were on a train heading back to Hastings. and I was worried about how we were gonna handle Pop, not Sid of course.

His head was dancing with all the wonders we'd seen and heard that day.

But it wasn't over yet! Not by a long shot. It was dark by the time the train finally rolled into Hastings. And we hadn't gone more than a few steps toward home when I heard something light and metallic hit the ground. I picked it up and got so mad at

Sid I could hardly stand it. It was the Sunshine Girl bottle cap and it made

me so crazy, I actually heard mad cackling Laughing in my head! I whirled on Sid and let him have it. I told him stealing a cap like that from Jim Wheatley was plain wrong, no matter how Low down Jim Wheatley might be. And Sid's whiney denial made me even madder. Even though Sid was stronger I think I could've and would've beat him up where he stood except Sid pointed out something I hadn't noticed. This Sunshine Girl couldn't have been Jim Wheatley's. It was practically mint condition, unlike Jim's!

And that's when I thought of that strange
laughter again
that I thought
I imagined and
sure enough
when I
mentioned
that to
Sid, he said
he thought he
heard laughing
too!

And we were
so caught up
in the incredible wonder of everything that
happened to us in one amazing day, we would
have caught it for sure from Pop if he
hadn't luckily been working late that night;
a thing that happened often enough.

Pop left a can of Chef Boyardee and
some other stuff for me to make dinner,
but Mildred already fed us even if we
could have thought of anything so mundane
as food after our day.

I think we would have gone right back over to the train station to look for more caps right then and there if Pop hadn't walked in with the usual six pack tucked under his arm.

So that was it for that night. But I'll tell you this. It was a long time before we got any sleep. We had a lot of plans to make and, lucky for us, the next day was Saturday.

Pop was still sleeping when we stole out the next morning and started scouting around the train station.

In practically no time at all we had four more Sunshine Girl caps! Even one for diet, the existence of which we never even suspected, and many others.

The trail of rare caps seemed to lead right toward the river. Right away we found several Coca-cola movie Queen caps of stars neither of us had ever heard of.

Some showed signs of rust like they might have been lying on the ground for a while, which was a pity 'cause we were finding caps to die for. Sid found a Miller girl in the moon cap earlier and sexier than any we'd ever seen. And right at river's edge, we even found a rusted stations of the cross, holy water cap!

We were so excited that by the time we got to the river, the sun was starting to set. The whole day had gone by so fast, it hardly seemed like even an hour!

And that's when I saw a cap fall right out of the sky into the Hudson River. I managed to reach in and grab it before it sank. It was another Sunshine Girl and I started to say, "Aw, it's nothin', just another Sunshine..."

Can you imagine how

jaded we were getting in just one day? That tells you something about it all right. But I didn't have much time to ponder 'cause, just then Sid pointed up to the sky and said "Look!"

Like I said the sun was setting but there was still light enough for us to see a red parrot flying out onto the river and still dropping more caps right into the Hudson, which was making Sid crazy; me too, if I'm going to tell the real truth. But I was also trying to keep that parrot in view. Dark as it was getting, I noticed that he seemed to be flying in the direction of the old Buccaneer. I couldn't be absolutely positive but the more I thought about it, the more I felt sure that had to be where that bird was heading. Even after I lost sight of him I heard, or thought I still heard that maniac parrot laugh like we heard the night before; so did Sid.

I wasn't exactly sure what our next move should be, but as we headed back with all our loot, we both caught sight of someone's old row boat and a plan for Sunday was already forming in my head before I even knew it.

Come Sunday I was itching to grab that old row boat and investigate the Buccaneer but I had enough  sense to realize that our best bet at it was to do a bunch of chores to keep Pop happy while Sid gloated over all our finds of the day before.

But, I could barely stand the waiting.

Finally, after doing the dishes from a mercifully early supper, Sid and me managed to steal away around seven thirty. It wasn't dark yet but I knew it wouldn't be long and we wanted to be ready.

Sid brought his backpack empty, to bring back caps in, except for two road flares

he found somewhere and what a blessing they turned out to be.

Remember what I said about there being no accidents? Well, we had one right off when the row boat started drifting off as soon as we pulled ourselves up into a couple of rotten port hole openings and if it wasn't for Sid's flares, we'd have been sunk. Even so, I sure had a sinking feeling as I saw that boat drifting off. There sure was no turning back.

But what we found, I knew was no accident but meant to be as sure as I know anything. It was a lot to take in, though.

In the middle of an old ship hold was a skinny maniac; hair streaked with gray down his back and a beard to match that reached a shrunken belly, that didn't look at all well fed.

He was laughing, throwing piles of bottle caps in the air and letting them fall all over him like an old miser with his gold coins in some fairy tale, and flying over him, laughing ever louder, was the red parrot, dropping even more old caps on him, then grabbing more and doing it again and again!

On the poor man's head, listing over to one side, was a crown with a crinkled edge. It looked like a big upside down bottle cap, except where a cap is empty to fit a bottle, there was a pillow cloth surface with five bottle caps, four

around the sides and one in the middle.
Sid's got it now. He'll be happy to show
it to you, I'm sure.

And speaking of Sid. Next I knew he'd
dropped (fell, I think) into the hold, and went
almost through the rotten floor boards
into another  hold that was mostly
filled with water
with fish
swimming in it.
He was still
holding on
for dear
life to the
rotten boards
and I don't
think
I would have
gone in there
otherwise
if he
wasn't
yelling
for
me to help.

See, I've been saving the worst part. Down at the end of the hold was a more or less mummified dead man! There was skin you could see bones right under and he was frozen into a cross-legged sitting position. In his open boney hands were rare old caps. But weirdest of all, his head, lighted by two candles grinned like a skull and in the sockets where his eyes should have been were rare Coke movie star caps that no one in living memory had ever seen before.*

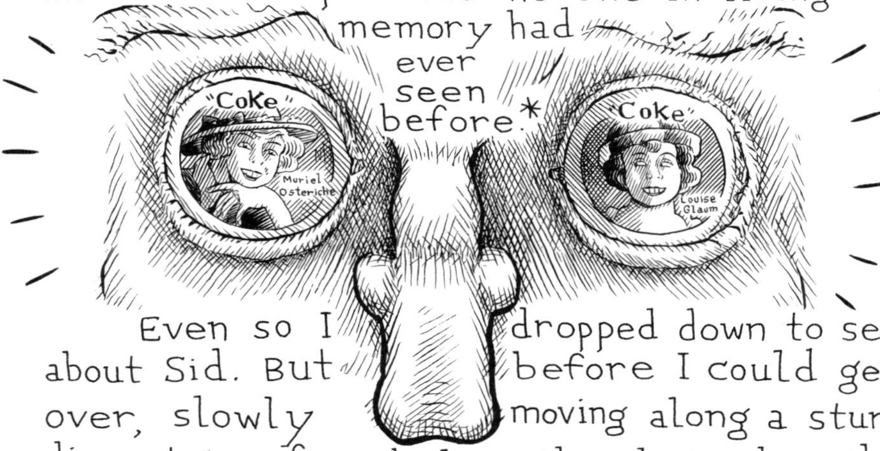
"CoKe"
Muriel Osteriche
"Coke"
Louise Glaum

Even so I dropped down to see about Sid. But before I could get over, slowly moving along a sturdier strip of wood along the ship's edge, the man spotted Sid, turned and grabbed his arm and started to yell,

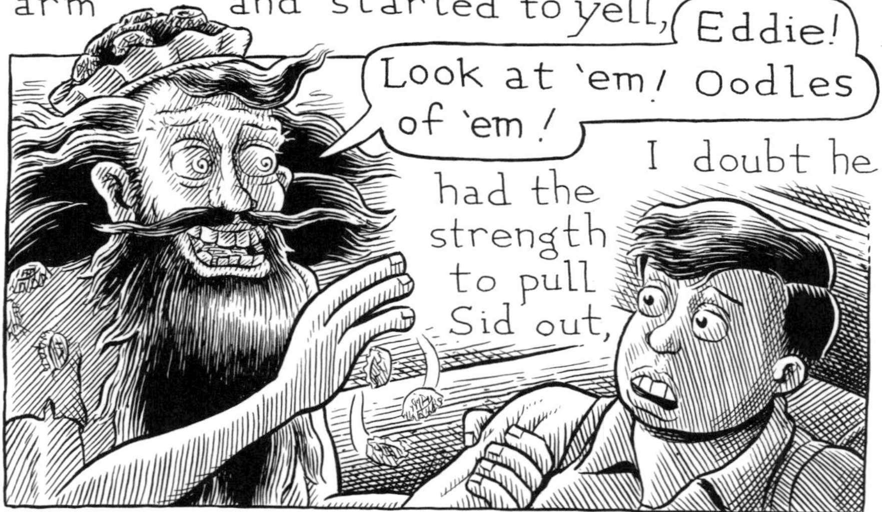
Eddie! Look at 'em! Oodles of 'em!

I doubt he had the strength to pull Sid out,

* Left cap, Muriel Ostriche. Right cap, Louise Glaum.

but I do believe he delayed Sid's falling all the way through the floor long enough for me to get there. How I managed to pull Sid back I still don't know but I did.

And meanwhile there's the crazy guy with the crown still calling Sid Eddie!

And then it hit me like lightning. It was our Uncle Gar and he was taking Sid for our Pop, 'cause without his glasses, which *did* fall into the brine below, Sid did look a lot like that picture Pop had of him and Gar as kids!

And that's when everything took on more momentum. We got out on the outside

of the ship somehow, being real careful 'cause that wood wasn't taking much weight and we managed to light those road flares Sid brought and soon we were yelling to beat the band. Even the parrot joined in.

And it wasn't much more than an hour, if that, before some police in a motor boat came and got us.

Well, that kicked off the nine day's wonder to end all nine days' wonders; at least in my life. And I don't think it's ever really stopped for Sid.

That sure was Uncle Gar and, at least at first, he cleaned up pretty good. He wasn't, in truth, much over thirty years old and with a shave and a hair cut, not too shabby. And seeing him and Pop together was worth everything and then some as far as I'm concerned. Gar seemed pretty lucid in those first

GAR!

days; I mean when you took into consideration what he'd been through. But what
I was really noticing was the change in Pop.
   He was like a new man, like the worries
of the world got taken off his shoulders.
Pop quit drinking and, best of all, he and Mom
got back together which is something I
never expected; talk about your
miracles!

Gar's
new
look

fixed
teeth

Gar was shaky for sure but managed to tell what happened quite a few times at that 'cause you never in your life saw so many reporters, the papers, local news CNN, you name it. And Gar spit out his strange story which was, back in seventy-

six, Gar and Ed, my Paw, had been doing a lot of looking at the burnt out site of Aaron Garnett's secret bottling plant 'til they just about gave up. But Gar still wanted to see if maybe there wasn't something they'd overlooked.

That last night in seventy-six Gar wanted Pop to go with him one last time but Pop wouldn't and was just sick about it when Gar went missing and everyone assumed he'd drowned.

Well, what happened is Gar found a basement room under the burnt ruins; found it by falling on his head into the damp room.

When he came to he was on that ship with Aaron Garnett! Aaron had been hiding out there with a big supply of Sunshine Soda he'd been taking there and storing little by little for several weeks before the Police raid on his plant and had been hiding out there ever since.

We never did find out how it was that he revisited the plant the night Gar fell or how Gar got to the Buccaneer but it happened. And they were living there together eating fish they'd catch and drinking all that Sunshine Soda, case after case, 'til it finally ran out. By that time they were in such an exalted state from all that L.S.D., they were like a couple of strange old holy men, or so Gar described it, 'til one day Aaron just slipped right out of his body in that same sitting position we found him in.

Gar insisted Aaron wasn't really dead at all and that he still talked with him all the time.

At first my theory was he was talking to that old Macaw, Noodles and he only thought he was still talking with Aaron because sometimes I do hear the two of them going at it.

And let's face it, there was something downright astonishing about the way that old bird of Aaron's led us to Gar.

Anyway, it did become increasingly apparent that outside of being all spruced up Gar never really was his old self again and less and less so as time went by. He sure didn't have any of his old bottle cap fever any more.

But he did like sitting with Pop. They'd watch TV together usually tapes of Gar's rescue

or maybe one of Pop's John Wayne movies. Didn't much matter really what they were watching. Pop was just so happy to be with Gar again and Gar would just be sitting there with a contented, far away look in his eyes.

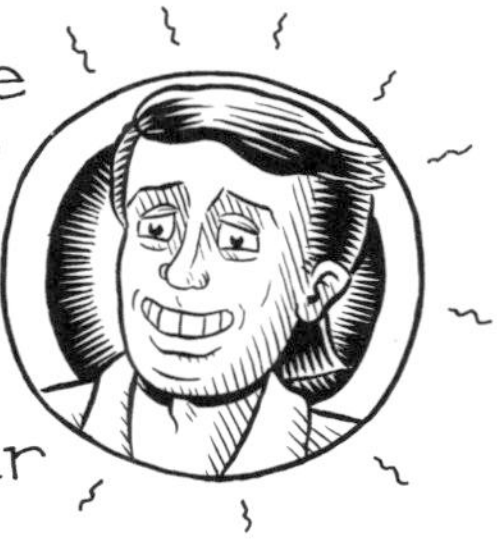

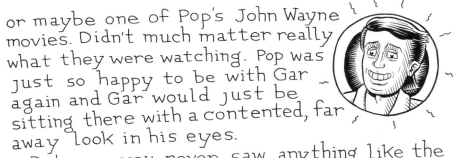

But, say, you never saw anything like the crown cap convention of 1993. Or maybe you heard about it. There was plenty of coverage on TV.

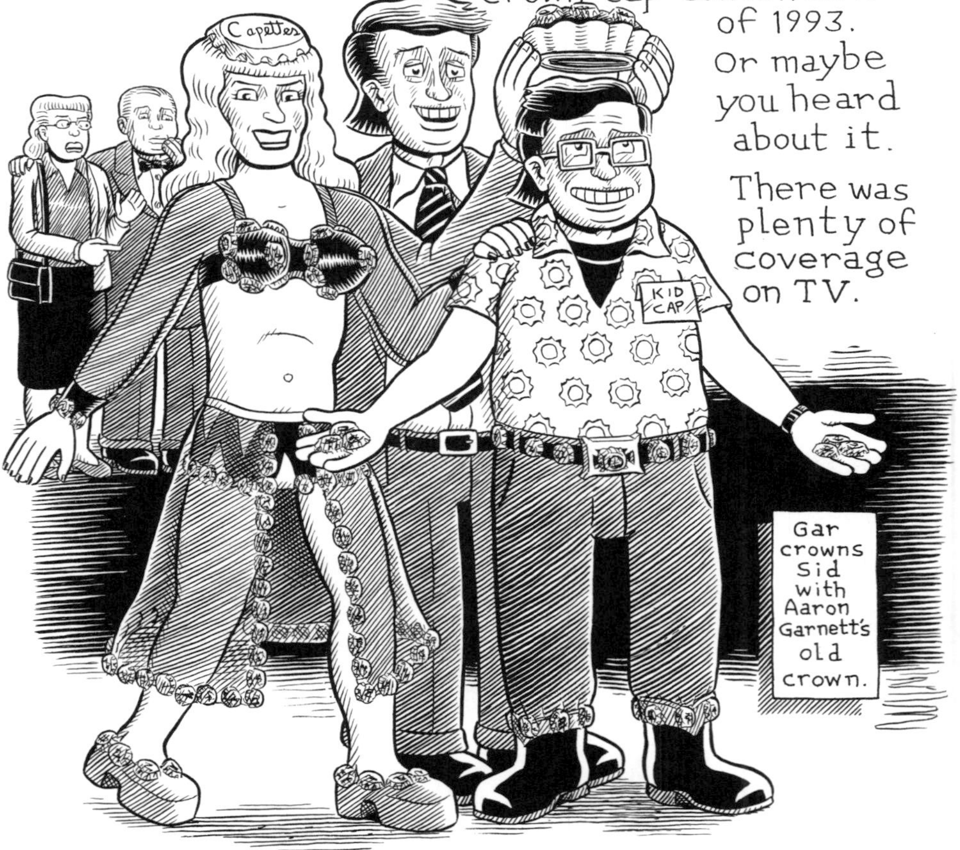
Capettes
KID CAP
Gar crowns Sid with Aaron Garnett's old crown.

No half empty old camera store that time.
It was two floors of the Jacob Javits Center
in New York City and Sid and me and Gar
were the guests of honor. There was a big
ceremony when Gar took that crown that
Aaron Garnett gave him and crowned Sid the
new crown cap king of, almost, the world.

Note: It was at this con that I first met Ellie. And on
the next few pages   are pictures I worked up from
photos and sketches   that I made there.   K.D.

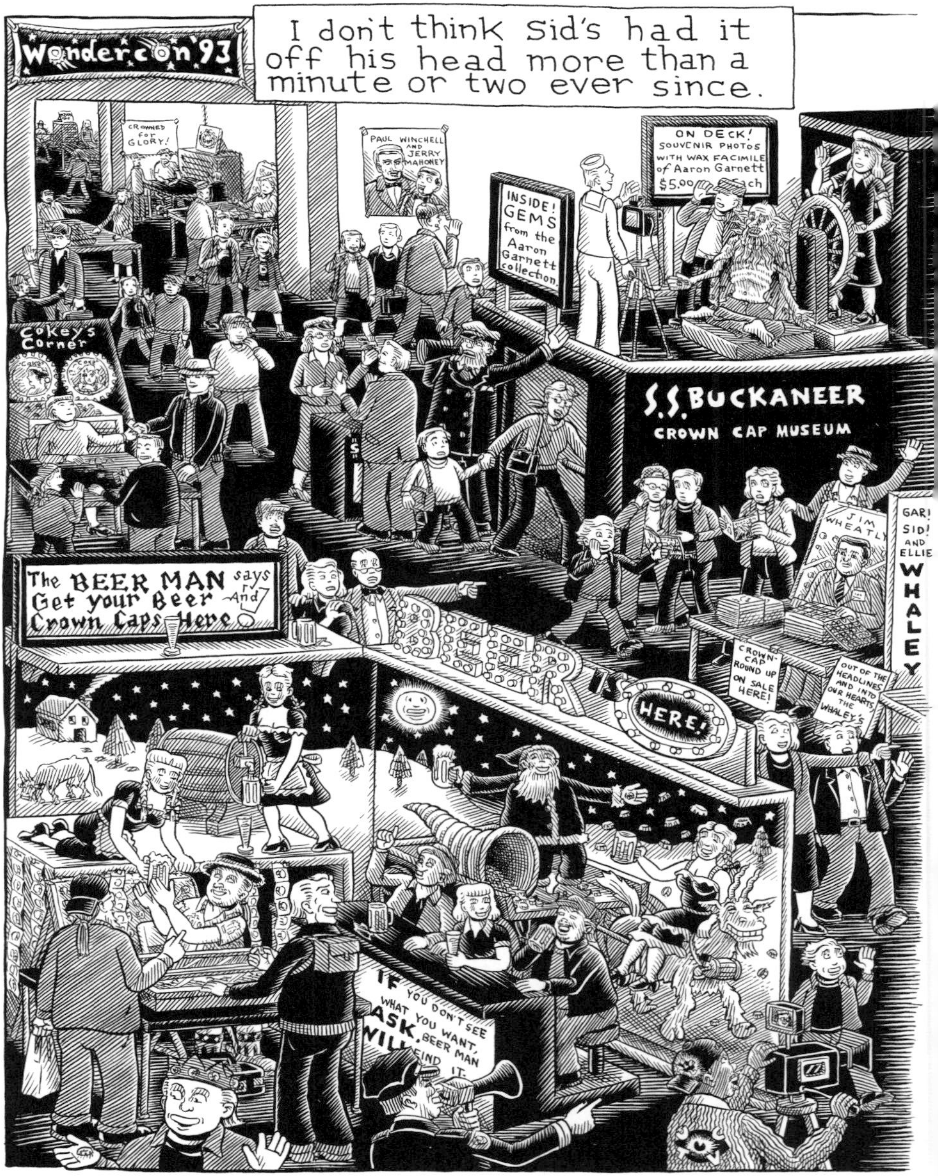
I don't think Sid's had it off his head more than a minute or two ever since.
Wondercon '93
CROWNED for GLORY!
PAUL WINCHELL AND JERRY MAHONEY
INSIDE! GEMS from the Aaron Garnett collection.
ON DECK! SOUVENIR PHOTOS WITH WAX FACIMILE of Aaron Garnett $5.00
Cokey's Corner
S.S. BUCKANEER
CROWN CAP MUSEUM
JIM WHEATLY
GARI SID! AND ELLIE WHALEY
The BEER MAN says Get your Beer And Crown Caps Here
CROWN-CAP ROUND UP ON SALE HERE!
OUT OF THE HEADLINES AND INTO OUR HEARTS THE WHALEY'S
HERE!
IF YOU DON'T SEE WHAT YOU WANT, ASK. BEER MAN WILL FIND IT.

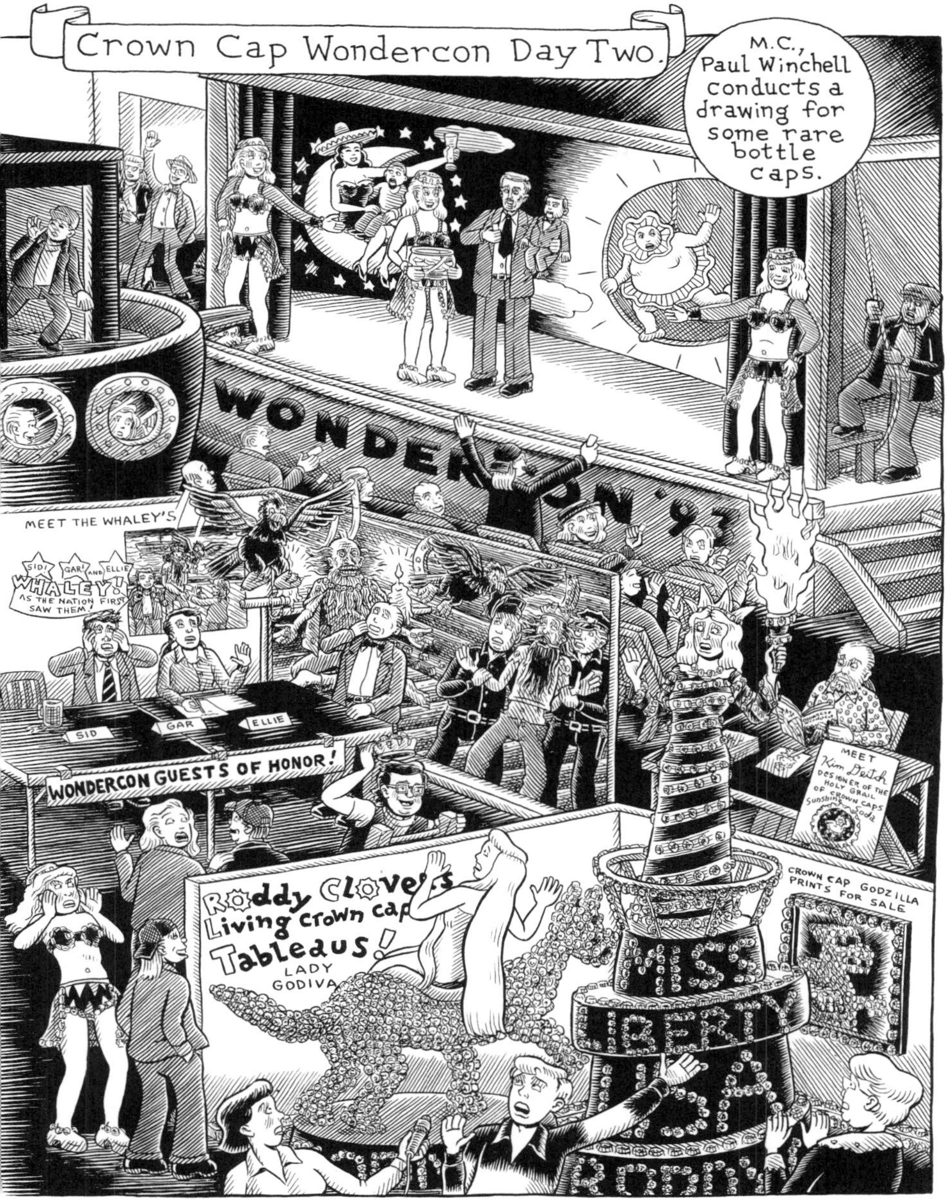

Crown Cap Wondercon Day Two.
M.C., Paul Winchell conducts a drawing for some rare bottle caps.
MEET THE WHALEY'S
SID! GAR! AND ELLIE WHALEY! AS THE NATION FIRST SAW THEM!
SID
GAR
ELLIE
WONDERCON GUESTS OF HONOR!
MEET Kim Deitch DESIGNER OF THE HOLY GRAIL OF CROWN CAPS Sunshine Soda
Roddy Clover's Living crown cap Tableaus!
LADY GODIVA
CROWN CAP GODZILLA PRINTS FOR SALE
MISS LIBERTY USA

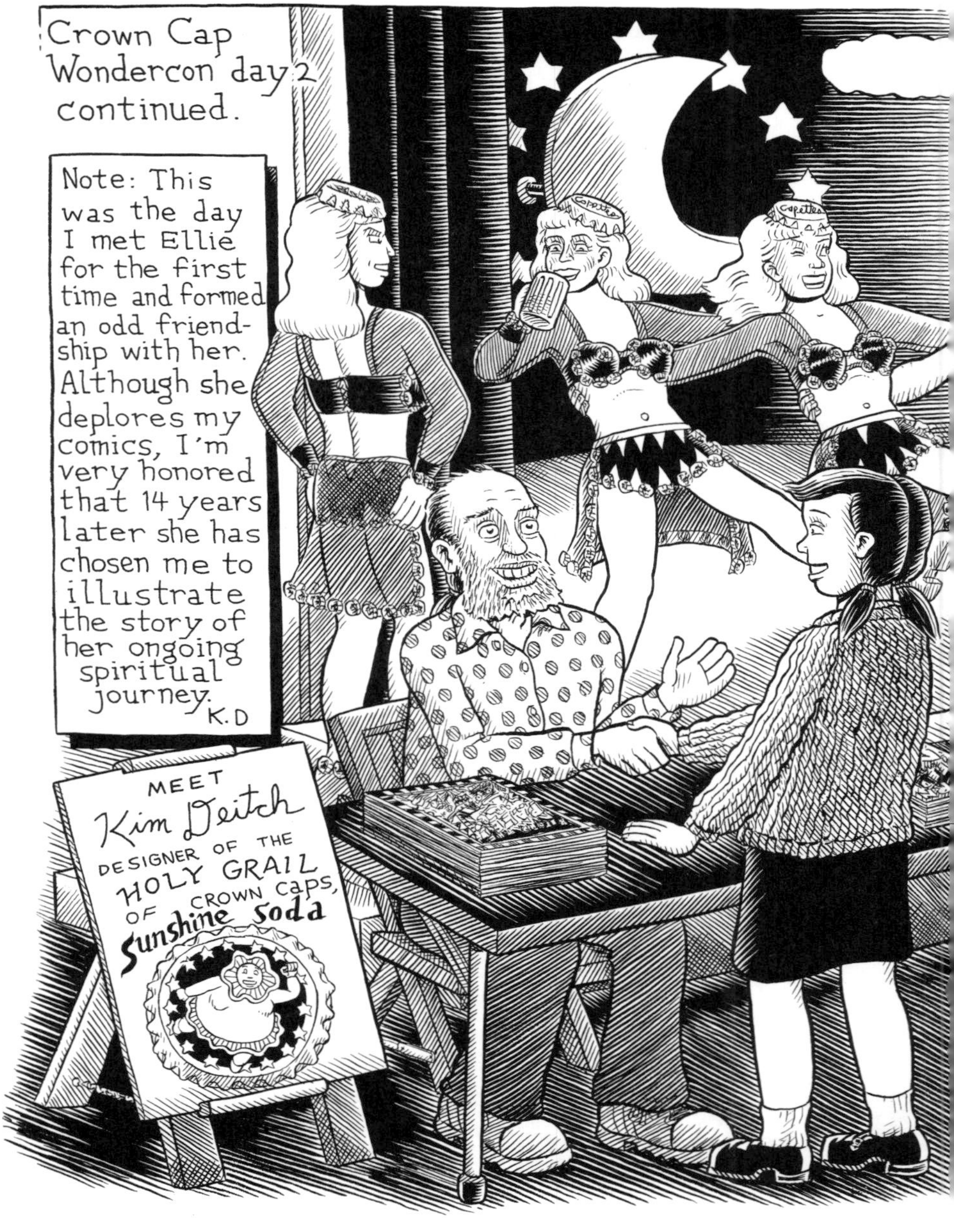
Crown Cap Wondercon day 2 continued.
Note: This was the day I met Ellie for the first time and formed an odd friendship with her. Although she deplores my comics, I'm very honored that 14 years later she has chosen me to illustrate the story of her ongoing spiritual journey. K.D
MEET Kim Deitch DESIGNER OF THE HOLY GRAIL OF CROWN CAPS, Sunshine Soda

SID'S BEER. ONE OF THE FIRST OF MANY.

You see, the whole thing got Sid flying so high I don't think he's ever really come down. It's sure to happen some day and of this you can be sure; I'll be there to catch him when he does.

Which may bring up a question you might be asking at this point. If Sid's the crown cap king how come I'm not the queen since I had as much to do with

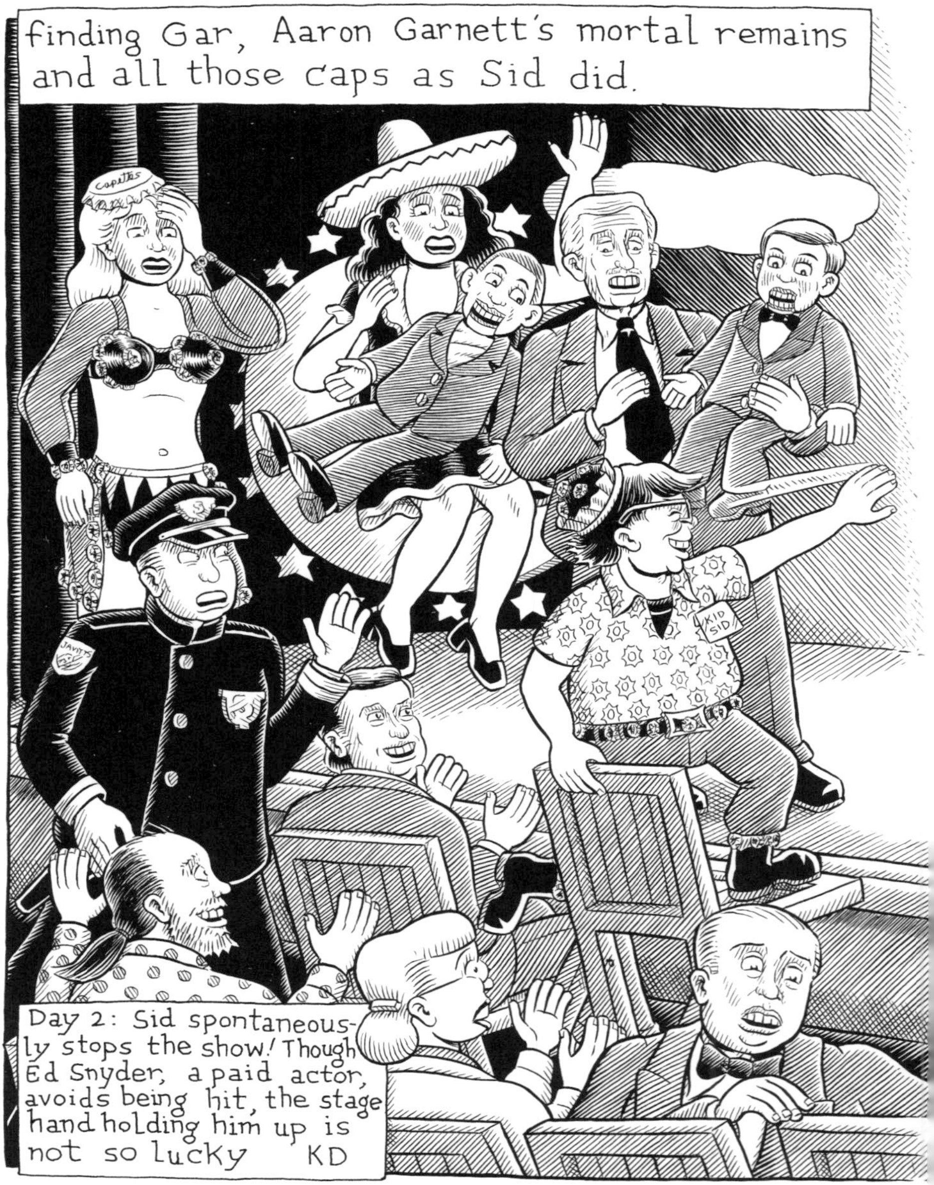
finding Gar, Aaron Garnett's mortal remains and all those caps as Sid did.
KID SID
Day 2: Sid spontaneously stops the show! Though Ed Snyder, a paid actor, avoids being hit, the stage hand holding him up is not so lucky KD

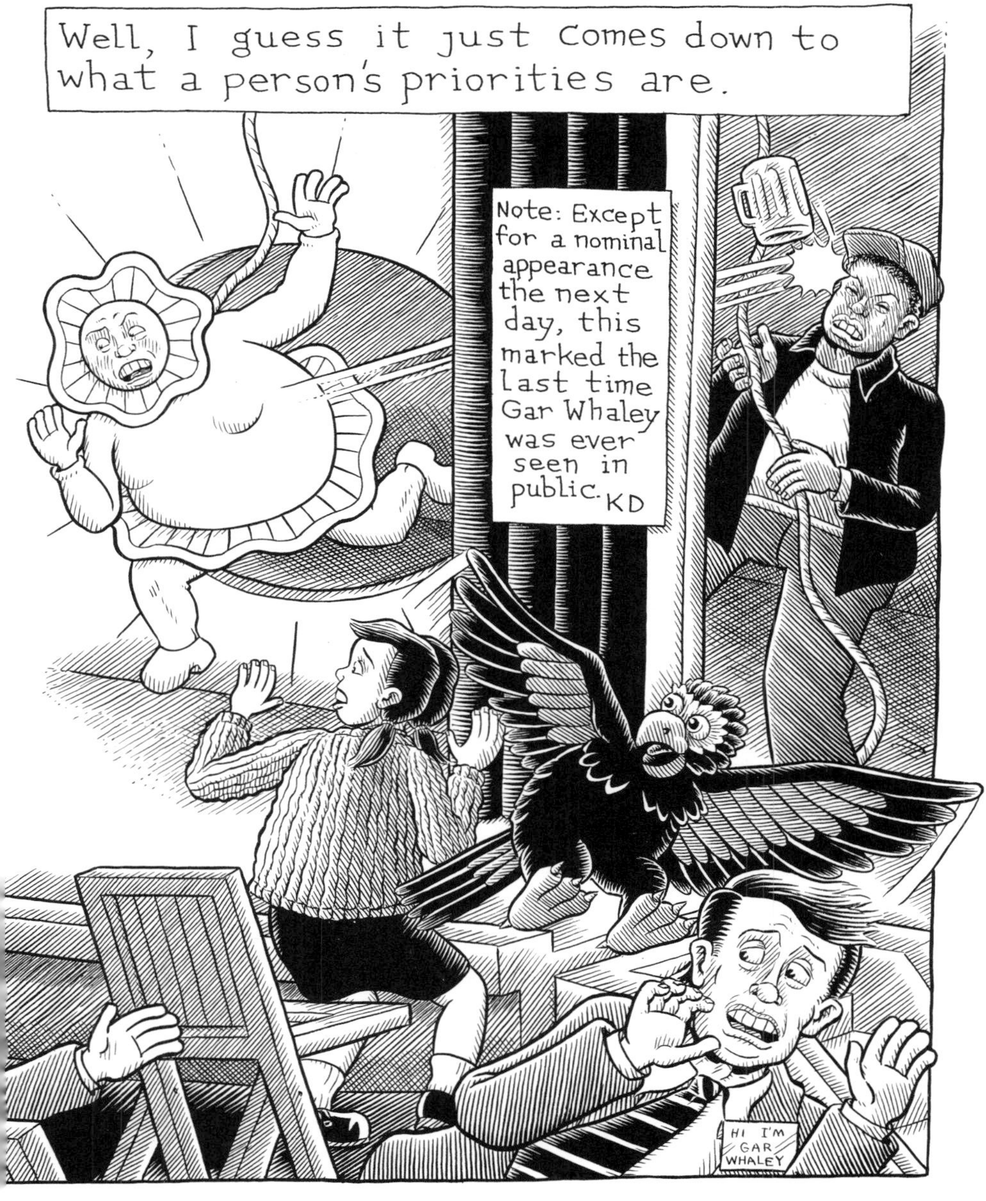

Well, I guess it just comes down to what a person's priorities are.
Note: Except for a nominal appearance the next day, this marked the last time Gar Whaley was ever seen in public. KD
HI I'M GAR WHALEY

I'll admit, at the beginning, I was as swept up in it all as anybody. But over time, especially after I saw Mom and Pop get back together,

Day 3: The Whaley family panel almost meets with disaster when Sid and Gar back out. However, even with two dubious last minute substitutions, it succeeds owing to Ellie's spontaneous and sincere presentation. KD

Gar just isn't cut out for the limelight.

I began to think maybe there was something more to living than just having a bunch of things.

That big con sure caused the value of the rarer caps to go right through the roof.

I took my share of the Aaron Garnett collection, mostly doubles Sid didn't need, and sold most of them to Jim Wheatley.

And boy did he cut a sad figure at that 1993 con; kind of wandering around trying to find his place at the the table. He sure wasn't going to be the crown cap king or any other kind of king. Anyway, he made this crazy offer to buy out my share. And against a lot of advice I was getting, I took it.

I will say now that I'm truly sorry I did. But not for the reason you're thinking; that I probably could have got a lot more money. No doubt I could have, but it got me enough

to buy this house and something laid away
to look after Sid, Gar and that old bird
Noodles.

No, the reason I'm sorry is I didn't
know that Jim Wheatley threw himself so
into debt borrowing (and stealing, apparently).
And I found out later that in the end he
had to sell off all his caps to hire lawyers and he died broke and alone a few
years ago.

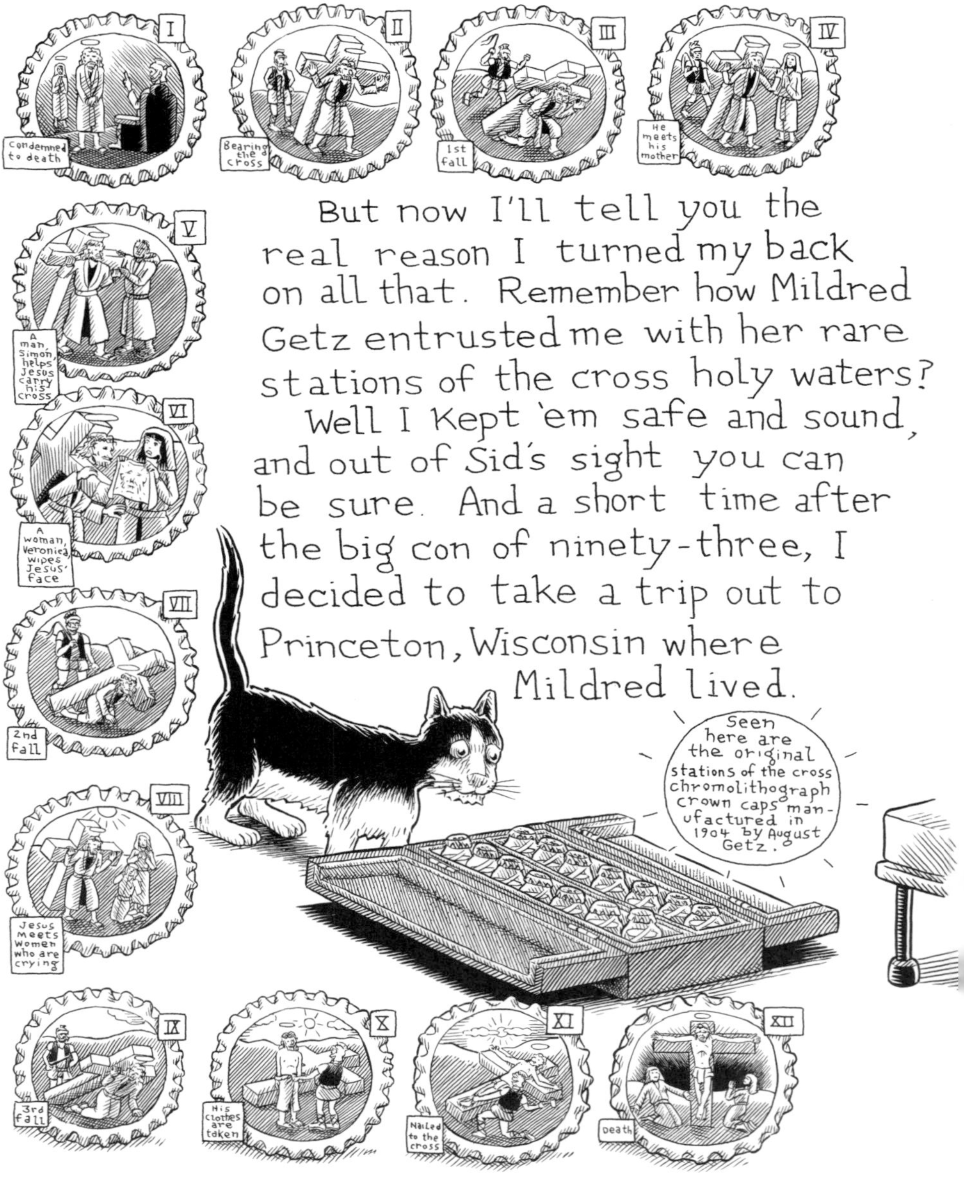
I
Condemned to death
II
Bearing the cross
III
1st fall
IV
He meets his mother
But now I'll tell you the real reason I turned my back on all that. Remember how Mildred Getz entrusted me with her rare stations of the cross holy waters?
Well I kept 'em safe and sound, and out of Sid's sight you can be sure. And a short time after the big con of ninety-three, I decided to take a trip out to Princeton, Wisconsin where Mildred lived.
V
A man, Simon, helps Jesus carry his cross
VI
A woman, Veronica, wipes Jesus' face
VII
2nd fall
Seen here are the original stations of the cross chromolithograph crown caps manufactured in 1904 by August Getz.
VIII
Jesus meets women who are crying
IX
3rd fall
X
His clothes are taken
XI
Nailed to the cross
XII
Death

And not a moment too soon. You see, Mildred was in the last stages of terminal lymphoma, a kind of cancer. In fact we didn't know it at the time but she was actually suffering from it when we first met her.

In spite of how weak she was she was mighty glad to see me. And even though it was almost time for school to start, Pop fixed it so I could stay with her during her final days.

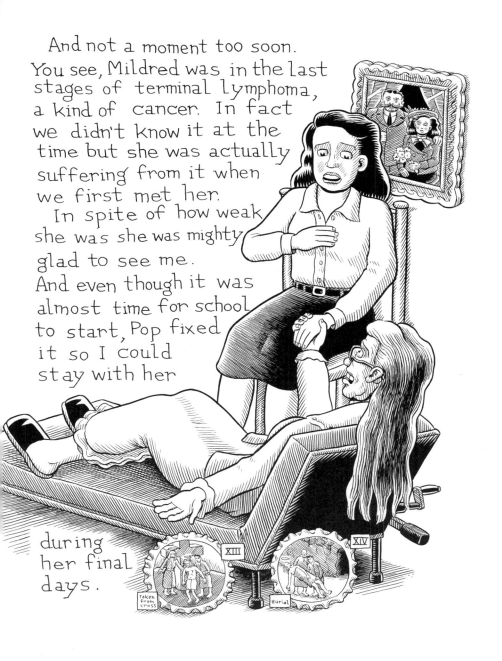

To my surprise, Mildred wouldn't take the holy waters back and I have them yet; the only crown caps I do now own.

But she did make one last request of me which was she wanted me to accept Jesus Christ as my lord and savior, which I did. Though I was already Catholic, I'd never really given much thought to real religion like I've got now. And it's worth more to me than any earthly goal; but we won't argue the point.

The fact is me and my minister out
here don't always see eye to eye on
every little detail of religion either.
You see, I've got to say I probably
picked up more insights about all that
from my so-called crazy uncle Gar.

When he's not just flat out
raving with that old red macaw, he
often drops some real pearls;
things he and Aaron saw in visions

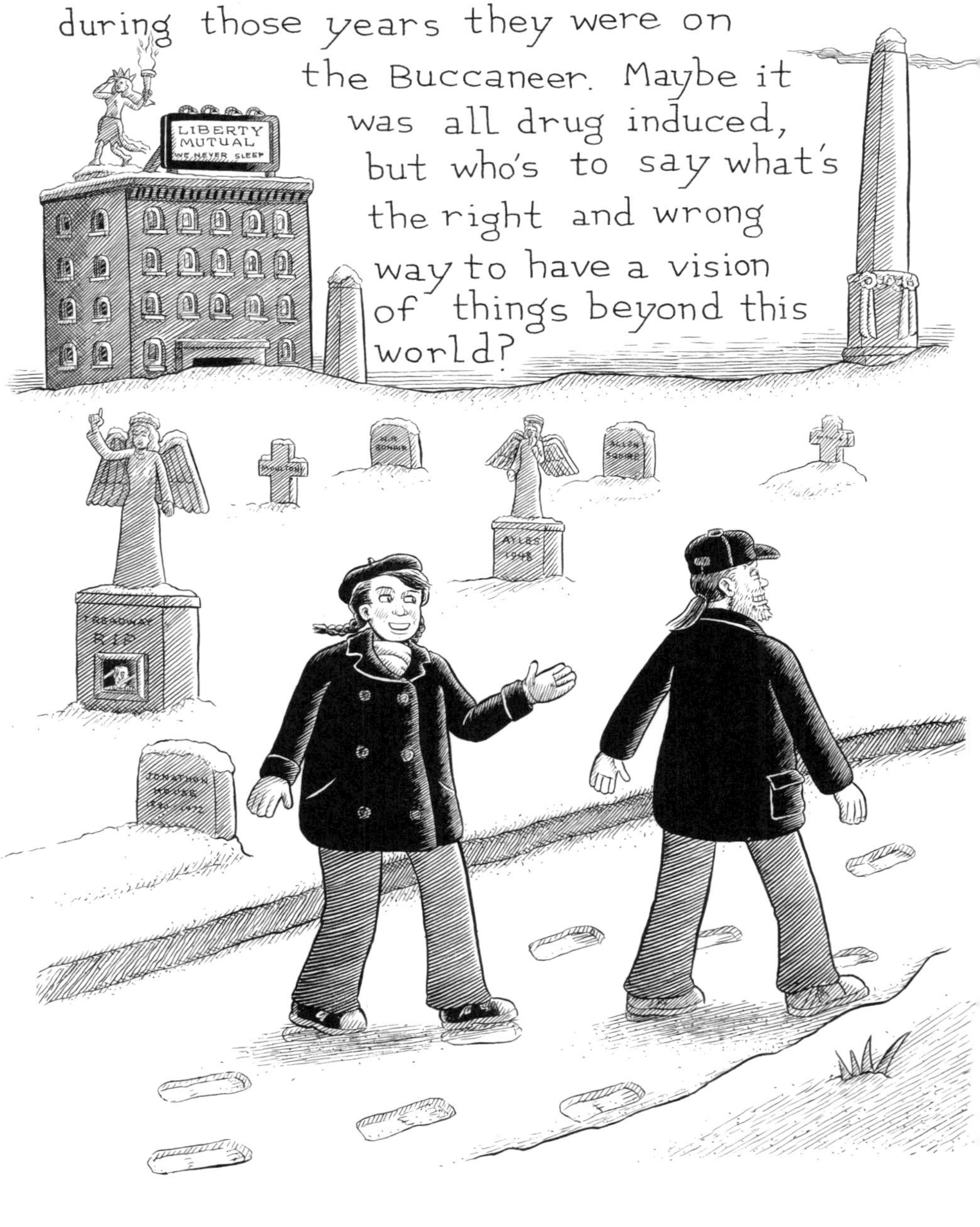
during those years they were on the Buccaneer. Maybe it was all drug induced, but who's to say what's the right and wrong way to have a vision of things beyond this world?
LIBERTY MUTUAL
WE NEVER SLEEP
RIP

Saint John the Baptist was madder than a hatter by all logical evidence and I can't help thinking that Aaron Garnett just may be the forerunner of our lord's return. Make no mistake. He is coming again. How do I know? Well, all the signs are out there and besides, I have my sources. You see, it took some wheeling and dealing with the board of health but I finally got a proper resting place for Aaron Garnett; not hidden away to be forgotten either. And I often go to visit him at the crypt I had built in our local cemetery.

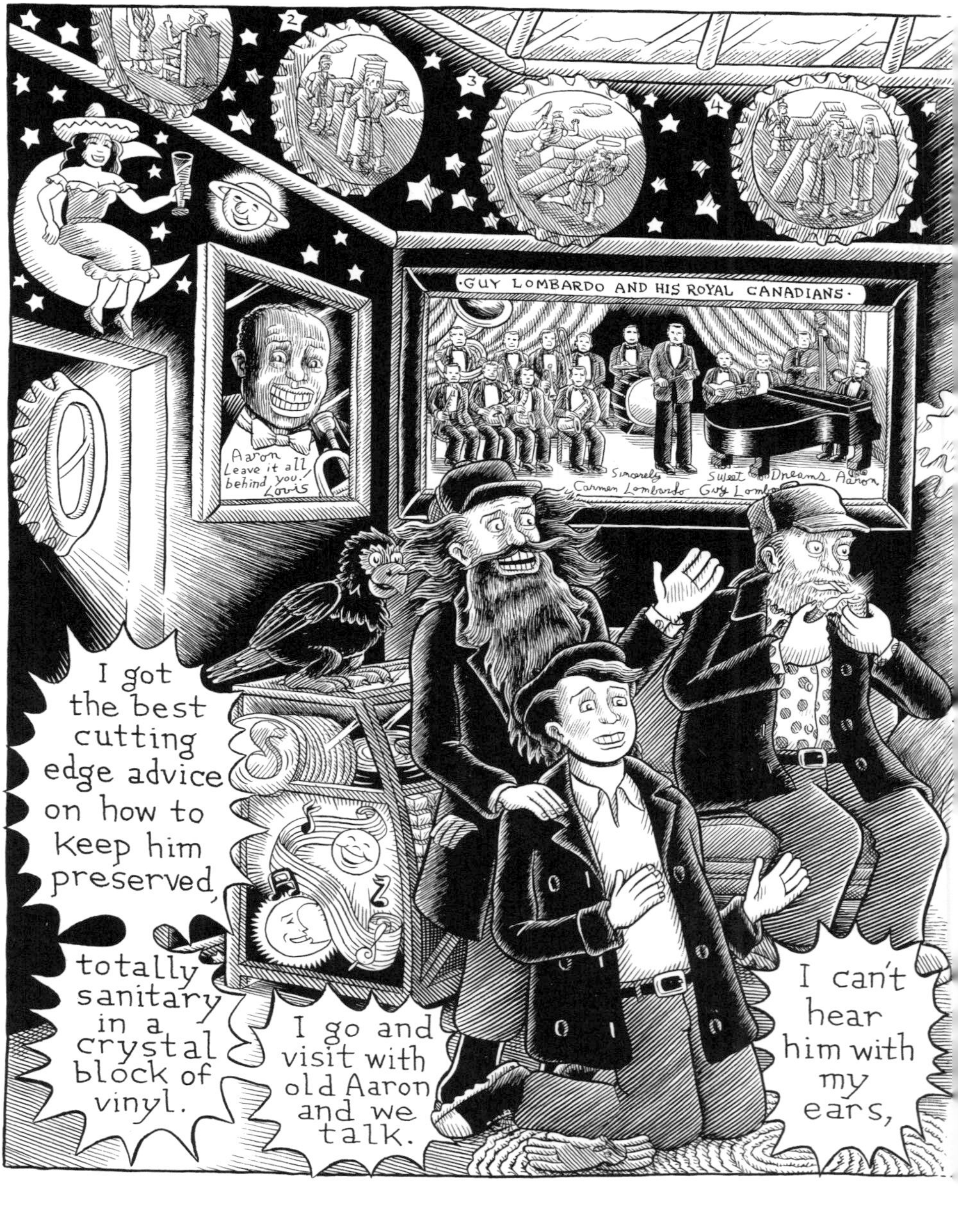
2
3
4
·GUY LOMBARDO AND HIS ROYAL CANADIANS·
Aaron Leave it all behind you! Louis
Sincerely Carmen Lombardo
Sweet Dreams Aaron
I got the best cutting edge advice on how to keep him preserved,
totally sanitary in a crystal block of vinyl.
I go and visit with old Aaron and we talk.
I can't hear him with my ears,

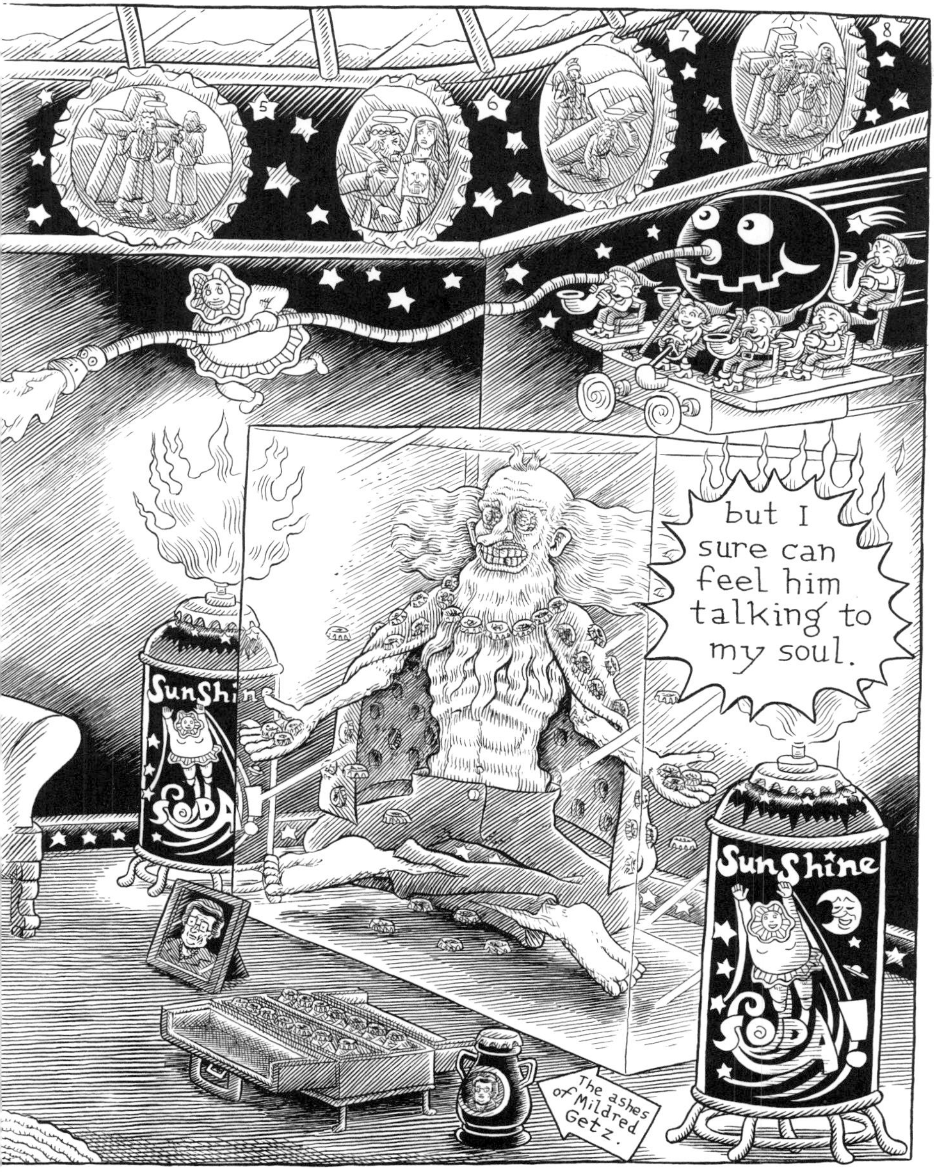
5
6
7
8
but I sure can feel him talking to my soul.
SunShine SODA
SunShine SODA!
The ashes of Mildred Getz.

*"Brahm shook as he stood in place, his legs would not
move even as the golem approached more closely."*

THE GOLEM

A TALE OF THE DARK AGES · · ·

By Seth Kallen Deitch and Simon Deitch

PROLOGUE

21ST CENTURY

Offenberg had been on worse digs, to be sure, but the work was still tedious and dirty even if it was a beautiful spring day. Eastern Europe was a far more pleasant environment than the Sahara, but dirt and sweat were everywhere in his business. The archeologist had come to Grôtnì in search of the lives of the everyday people of late antiquity. Yes, the doings of kings and armies shaped the political landscape, but the story of humanity is also told in how we have prepared our meals, the clothing we have worn and the games we have played to entertain ourselves.

Twelve hundred years ago a town had stood here on a great market road where a small but cosmopolitan community grew and thrived. The people here farmed and played and loved. It wasn't the kind of archaeology that made the popular press, but it was vital to the understanding of humanity's journey and Frederick Offenberg was one of this branch of learning's leading investigators.

With a soft brush he swept away at a small patch of brown earth that was one of many marked off with a grid of strings suspended a few inches above the ground by wooden dowels. Each square was one meter on a side. A short distance away, Ronald, a graduate student, was cleaning off objects on a makeshift table. As Offenberg swept, five smooth stones were revealed. They sat in an odd pattern. After more dirt was cleared he saw that they were five fingers of a very large stone hand.

By the end of the day, he had fully revealed the hand. It was slightly more than half a meter from the tip of the middle finger to where it was broken off just past the wrist joint. Beside it sat a wooden chest. When the chest was opened, it was discovered to contain number of remarkable documents.

From the *Associated Press* newswire:

COULD IT BE THE LEGENDARY GOLEM?

Thursday. Recent discoveries at a site near Grôtnì in the former Yugoslavian republic of Croatia have been connected to the ancient stories of the Mysterious "Golem" of Jewish lore. They include an enormous stone hand measuring approximately twenty inches from wrist to fingertip and some deteriorating scrolls. A few of the scrolls seem to make up one of the earliest known alchemical grimoires. A "grimoire" is a manual and log of alchemical or magical processes. The name comes from the same root word from which we get the word "grammar." Two of the scrolls are of special interest in that they are more personal documents. Early decipherment of the scrolls hints at a previously unrecorded tale of a golem, a living, in this case stone, giant. This account dates several centuries earlier than any known from Europe thus far.

Frederick Offenberg, the leader of the expedition that uncovered the relics, was unwilling to speculate on the story's authenticity, saying only that it represents a telling of this piece of Jewish mythology considerably older than previously known.

The artifacts have been dated to approximately 750 a.d. during the reign of Byzantine Emperor Constantine Copronymous (Constantine V).

The golem tale best known to the general public involves the rabbi Judah Lowe of Prague who supposedly created a golem of clay to defend the Jewish community from the so-called "blood libel" wherein the Jews were believed to use the blood of Christian babies to make their matzos in spite of the fact that Jews are forbidden by religion to consume blood, let alone human blood. That this story was ever able to take hold in the popular imagination merely illustrates the degree of anti-Semitism that was rampant in Europe in those times.

"Recent discoveries include an enormous stone hand measuring approximately twenty inches from wrist to fingertip."

In his office at the University, Offenberg labored to translate the documents. One of them was written in Byzantine Greek and was fairly straightforward, the other was composed in a combination of Latin and Hebrew that had been rendered in a number of obscure writing systems, with Enochian, an alphabet favored by alchemists and other mystics, most prominent among them. The Grimoire was composed in several different languages including a couple with which Offenberg was unfamiliar.

The Greek scroll looked to have been once longer and had been spliced together with large gaps in the text. Even so, the story it told was remarkable.

CHAPTER 1

Tenth day of June, year 4501, or 750 of Jesus Christ

Uncle has said that I should keep a daily record of my life because it builds good discipline and will improve my writing skills. He also said that even my young life can add to the wisdom of the world.

I am Jemma, the daughter of Moishe and Tovah. My parents were killed last autumn by a highwayman who was outraged to discover they were poor Jews and had nothing for him to take. I was left an orphan and made my way to the house of my Uncle Raveh who is my Father's older brother. I thought that he might take me in because I was fourteen years old and already knew most of the womanly arts and he had no wife. He would welcome someone to cook for him, clean his house and mend his clothing.

He welcomed me not for those things but because he had loved his brother and said he would love me as he had loved him. Any fears of abuse or disregard by a strange relative had been assuaged.

Uncle married and then became a widower when he was almost as young as I and has never remarried. He has lamented that it is a terrible thing that there is no woman to guide me through these next few years on the road to womanhood. I have always seen myself as a simple and humble being and no great enigma, but Uncle sees me otherwise. For Uncle Raveh, life itself is a mystery that may be delved into and discovered, but to him the life of a woman is a mystery beyond all depth.

"...an old watchtower that he had converted for his studies and experiments."

"Uncle had loved his brother and said he would love me as much as he had loved him."

My life with Uncle Raveh has been wonderful. He is not rich, but far better off than my father was, owning a sizable property north of Grotinion with a comfortable cottage, a barn and an old watchtower that he has converted for his studies and experiments. He is a very learned man and can read and write at least ten languages, half of which I have never heard of! He practices an art called *alchemy* that he says is part science and part discipline of the spirit. It is said that the great work of alchemy is the transformation of base metals into gold, but uncle cares not about such matters. He says that he seeks the secret of life itself! All I know is that he reads many books and writes quite a bit, has strange visitors from time to time and performs experiments that can emit fumes so strong that the eyes of Satan himself would water!

Uncle did one experiment not long after I came to live with him where he attempted to restore life to a dead rat (as if there were not already too many live ones!). He prepared a special fluid in one of his furnaces and put only a few drops of it on the rat. To my astonishment, the rat rose up and scurried about the table-top, but after a moment, it stopped and shook itself a few times. Without warning, the rat suddenly exploded into a cloud of dust!

If this all sounds very strange, well, it *is* compared to my former life, but Uncle Raveh and I are a happy family. In the evenings Uncle tells me wonderful stories of distant times and places.

Learning is the most important thing in the world so far as Uncle is concerned. Every day I must devote an hour to the study of the Torah, three hours before sunset on the day before the Sabbath. As well as Greek, Hebrew and Bulgur, which I must know, Uncle wants me to learn Latin, Gothic and Arabic! As well as the Torah, he wants me to have at least passing knowledge of the testaments of the Christians and the holy text of the Mohamedans, even the strange pagan ways of the people of Hindustan! Women are rarely scholars and *never* merchants so I don't know what he expects me to become. Perhaps I can at least teach my skills to others. He says, *"We live in an age of ignorance and want, my child, but the possessor of knowledge has riches beyond measure."*

I also have many chores. Since I have come here, Uncle has had me take complete charge of the house so that he can spend more time with his studies and his letters. The cleaning and the cooking are of no great consequence to me. I love to cook and I naturally prefer a clean house. I have to make sure the goats and chickens stay well fed and out of trouble. I also help in the laboratory, which is easy for I have only to do exactly what Uncle tells me and otherwise stay out of the way. The part of my chores that I am less fond of is going to market by myself in Grotinion. When I

"The part of my chores that I am less fond of is going to market by myself in Grotinion."

go to market, the young men all stare at me in a most disconcerting manner! Even two years ago I never suffered such scrutiny. It is as if I have somehow become a kind of mythic creature that none of the boys know how to speak to in a sensible manner. As if the boys my own age are not confusing enough, there is also Brahm, the legionary. Actually, I don't think he is a legionary any more. There is something that is simply wrong about him, a taint that will not come out. I believe that the legion decided that they would do better without him amongst their numbers so now all he has to do is idle about the town. He has spoken to me on occasion, he has a Gothic accent, but mostly he stares at me from across the market square as if he sees me as he would a deer he was stalking. On the few occasions that he has spoken to me, he has seemed to be fascinated by the Mogen David star I wear on a chain around my neck, a gift from my father. I know he is not a Jew, but he has some sort of fascination with us. I wonder if he believes the many slanders against God's chosen people.

Twentieth day of June

Uncle has houseguests that he has put up in the tower. They have their meals in the house with us and I have had much opportunity to practice my Latin, for that is the language in which they converse. One of them is an Egyptian Jew called Abramelin. There is a Saracen called Al-Hazared who twitches and laughs for no reason at all some times, perhaps he is mad. There is a mage from Britannia that Uncle simply calls "the Druid" who has an apprentice a few years older than me named Mhurlyn. My Latin is not poor, and yet the bulk of their conversation is impossible for me to understand for it deals with very arcane aspects of alchemy. They have gathered together and made many notes on the big wax tablet in the laboratory.

They shall take their leave soon, and that is good because I think their presence has agitated Uncle Raveh and the bishop would expel us from the land, or worse if he were found to be harboring Pagans and Mohammedans. Being a Jew in this Christian empire is difficult enough without being a Jew who consorts with the foreign infidel.

I went again to the market today and was cornered by Brahm. He had had quite a bit of wine judging from his aroma. He offered me a half-follis coin to visit him in his room at the tavern. He asked why I was offended when I told him to leave me alone. "Are not all Jewesses whores?," he asked mockingly. He is an odious creature, and I have heard he is a thief as well. I must take care and watch out for him in the future.

Sixth day of July

The foreign visitors departed over a week ago and Uncle has barely left the tower. Twice now, I have had to go and wake him where has fallen asleep at his work table and urged him to go to bed! I fear for his health should he continue to work this hard.

The object of his labor is a bezoar stone that he obtained from the Saracen Al-Hazared who in his turn obtained it from a sage in Persia who is said to have received it from the hands of a trader from the distant land of Altay who had brought it traveling with a caravan by way of the fabled Silk Road from the remote city of Chan-gan in the empire of the Tang that is called Cathay! Uncle thought that with the proper process, this stone could bring forth life!

He had kept it enclosed in a retort of clear glass over a bed of glowing coals for many days and would bring it to a window on certain nights to allow light from the planet Jupiter fall upon it! After a time, the stone started to sweat out a dark fluid that dripped from the retort and uncle carefully preserved. He removed the stone from the retort and placed it in another piece of glassware, a large sphere and pored over it the black fluid to which he had added yellow bile from an ox and the powdered root of the *mandragora* plant. He then exposed it to the light of the planet Saturn. Over the fire, the surface of the stone started to show cracks as it absorbed the fluid. I admit that my curiosity was peaked and I asked Uncle Raveh what was to happen. "*If I have done everything correctly, if I have followed every step to the letter and if I have kept my spirit sufficiently pure during the process, then life will be born here today!*"

The stone suddenly crumbled and amidst the broken pieces was a little man curled up like a new-born baby. He was perfect in almost every detail. Uncle removed the glass from the fire and placed it in a stand on his worktable. After a time, the little man stood up and looked about in curiosity. He was a funny little

"He was a funny little creature with a big head.
There were stubby little horns on his forehead."

creature with a big head. There were stubby little horns on his forehead and one of his legs ended in a cloven hoof. Uncle removed him from the glass and set him on the tabletop.

The creature babbled in some unknown tongue and there was a look in his eye that filled me with unease. Not so with Uncle Raveh. He was filled with joy! He had engendered life from non-life!

21ˢᵀ CENTURY

It had been a long night and Offenberg had fallen asleep on his office couch. The strange diary of the alchemist's niece had proven to be so compelling that he had worked himself to exhaustion. It was nine a.m. when he was roused by tapping on his office door. He admitted Ronald as he rubbed sleep from his eyes.

Ronald made neither greetings nor apologies. "I have a preliminary decipherment of the Enochian scroll!" He stuck a yellow legal pad in front of Offenberg's face. "It's written in the Enochian script, but the language is Latin!"

Oftenberg went over to the desk and found his glasses. He then sat down and started to read. *Ravinius Magnus sum, liber ille viginte-sexus...*

CHAPTER 2

I am the great Ravinius, this book is the twenty-sixth volume of my notes and personal musings. In the year 4501 of the reign of the ineffable **_GOD_**, my researches into the nature of life, the most glorious of **_HIS_** creations have finally begun to bear fruit.

I sought the council of my brothers in the alchemical craft for what they might suggest for paths to pursue to achieve my goal. Abramelin suggested the formula and the rays of which planets to invoke. The Druid had the proper herbs or was able to tell me where to find them. The Saracen had the bezoar stone that would prevent the poisons from accumulating and thus killing the creature before it was even born. Thus, having followed the process which I have recorded in a detailed grimoire, I have brought forth a true and living homunculus! The creature seems to be more than merely animated earth and yet less than a complete soul. I only hope that he will be a proper tool to gain a more perfect understanding of the process of life.

The creature has proven to be worse than useless as a servant. Before I caged it, it wrought no end of havoc in the household, breaking dishes, setting things to flame, terrorizing the cat and defecating in places calculated to raise my ire. Now it sits forlornly in an old birdcage incessantly tapping with its hoof. If I do not destroy it, I fear it shall do so for eternity for I know not if it is mortal. I now see in its eye that it is animated by a malign spirit for not once in the process of its creation was the most holy name of **_GOD_** invoked.

I am at a crossroads in my study of life. I have made this wicked little thing but it has an evil soul and I cannot create a pure soul in the manner of **_GOD._**

Perhaps there might be a way to animate matter with only the germ of a soul that might have potential to develop one under my guidance. The soul comes from essence in the universe and is drawn into creatures that have bodies grown from the four elements of Air, Earth, Water and Fire. I wonder if a creature of not all the elements, perhaps only one element, might be brought into being.

Surely **_GOD_** knows of my musings and has sent help in the form of an old associate. I had gone to town to order some special pottery and glassware for my workshop when I saw him enter the town square with his three great wagons. Each wagon was heavily loaded and creaked with every motion even though they were particularly sturdily made to bear large amounts of weight. Two wagons were drawn by a team of four huge draft horses each and the third by a team of eight. The wagons were managed and guided by five slaves who in themselves appeared to have come from the four corners of the world. Atop the cargo of the largest

"Before I caged it, it wrought no end of havoc in the household."

wagon stood its master, Borah, the Macedonian stone cutter! He spotted me and called out to me with a hearty bellow "Ravinius Magnus! Raveh the Jew! I salute you, old friend!" and leapt down from the top of the wagon — for him quite a leap, for though Borah might have been mighty of muscle, he was short of stature, coming only to the height of my own chin. He trotted up to me and we embraced.

"What brings you this way, my friend?" I asked.

"I came north to seek *God's Forge*, the place where some of the Goths have told

"The Pyramids and the Sphinx still stand almost as good as new."

that the all the life of the world was made."

He then told me of a wondrous myth:

In the long night before the first dawn, God the creator labored at his forge beating out the shapes of all of the world's creatures. As he did his workshop became crowded with animals of all kinds. Great and small, they were soon to be sent out to populate the world upon the breaking of the first dawn. One of the creations, a bat, sought to be the world's master, the most powerful of beasts. The bat was small and had light bones. He had no hope of ruling the world when some of the other mighty beasts of God's creation existed! The bat conceived a plan that would make him the mightiest creature in all creation. He spilled out the coals from the forge upon the other beasts and they all died and became ashes. Seeing this, God sought to punish the bat, and God cast the bat out into the world before the dawn to dwell forever in the darkness and be the messenger of misfortune forever more. God forged new beasts and birds and man and set them all upon the Earth at the first dawn and the world was born. The pile of slag and ashes that

was God's first creations became a very special quarry that we have named Forge of God and in that stone we may see shadows of the bones of the creatures that never were and fearsome monsters some say are best forgotten.

Borah told me that the stone from that quarry was rumored to have special, subtle properties and he had wanted to obtain some to create a statue with.

That was when it struck me. This was the single element! Could I make a living creature only of earth? The stone of God's Forge might just be more amenable to such a transition.

I invited Borah to stay with me and camp his wagons and slaves on my land. I showed him the homunculus which he instantly saw for what it was, both brilliant success and bitter failure.

Borah fascinated little Jemma with tales of the places he had been and the things he had seen. He went on and on about the great works of sculpture and masonry. His father had taken him on a tour when he was a youth to see the wonders of the world. Once there had been seven but now there were only four.

The Pyramids and the Sphinx still stand almost as good as new and I swear that they will stand for all time, for so massive are they that the trump of doom will sound before wind and water shall bring them to the Earth and no act of man can ever shake such a foundation. The Colossus at Rhodes is still there, but fallen from an earthquake yet Helios is still mighty in repose. The tomb of old Mausollus still stands at Halicarnassos, though it is in poor repair and many of the statues have vanished. The celebrated Lighthouse at Alexandria yet stands in its full glory and still guides ships home. It is so high that it may be seen long before anything else appears on the horizon when a ship is at sea, for it is the tallest of any of the works of man. Its mirror is so finely polished and so elegantly curved that, if the day is bright enough, it could be used to set to fire the decks of invading ships!

On seeing these great wonders, I exclaimed to my father that these surely must be the work of God! 'No", he told me, "they are proof that there is nothing that man cannot achieve given strength, patience and the will to do it!'

While I was entertained by Borah's tales, Jemma was utterly transported by them. Her young imagination was fired by the narrative and by the sketches he drew on his tablet. Borah was an artist of great power who not only was a master of stone, but also drew marvelous pictures. He had repaid me for food and board once in the past by producing the most meticulous diagrams for my master grimoire. He was the only person beside myself I ever allowed to add a pen stroke to those pages.

With Borah, I discussed my work in detail, for he was a remarkably educated man and had many insights. Indeed, he had long been aware of and understood the underlying quest of my great effort. He did not disappoint me on this visit. He made a slave bring to him a small clay tablet, about the size of my hand. It was covered on both sides with wedge-shaped impressions, the ancient language of Babylon. Good old Borah! He knew that I was forever seeking such curiosities and had made certain that this one should find its way to me!

Borah said,

I obtained this document from one of the men who was building foundations for the new city of Baghdad. They regard artifacts of the Pagan past as valueless in their new Mohammedan world. May their trash become your treasure, for this tablet tells of the way to bring life to objects of the Earth. This shows the path by which a dead thing may become alive!

What incredible luck! That such a thing would fall into my hands. Surely **_GOD_** must will this! It was at the moment that this realization hit me that the homunculus chose to start laughing at me from his cage. I have grown to loathe that little monster but cannot yet bring myself to destroy it, for as of now, it is my singular success.

21ˢᵀ CENTURY

Offenberg looked up from the pad. "That's all you have?"

"Just the beginning. Now that I have the general concept of his cipher, the rest of the transliteration should come quickly enough."

Offenberg dismissed his assistant and roused himself to go in search of breakfast.

Returning well fed and with a cup of Dunkin' Donuts coffee at hand, he again set himself to the Greek scroll which was the diary of the young girl.

Chapter 3

Nineteenth day of July

Things have become quite exciting since Master Borah has come to stay with us! He has decided that he will make a great statue for Uncle Raveh right here in the tower. I write in the house today, for Master Borah's slaves are assembling a winch by which a huge block of stone may be lifted into one of the high rooms of the tower. Once it is completed, it will take a whole day to move the stone. Uncle Raveh has learned of how the Babylonians used to bring wood and clay and stone to life and he believes that he can do it too.

Twenty-fourth day of July

Master Borah has started to fashion a statue of a man from the great stone. He looks like an Egyptian slave, only bigger than any man I have ever seen, a mighty giant! I am amazed at the speed with which he works. I would have thought that it would take a month or more to hew the form of a man from that great block of stone, but his form, in outline if not detail, is already quite plain after only three days.

Uncle Raveh says that the stone giant is called "GOLEM" and that God shall place a spirit in it and it will serve us. He says that he will carve upon his forehead the name of an angel and that name shall be the power he serves.

As Master Borah cut away at the stone, I picked up some of the broken chips.

What wondrous stone it is, for it contains shells and bones, but they are shells and bones carven from stone! How did they get there? Who made them? Master Borah told me the tale of God's Forge and with such proof before me, I know that there must at least be *some* truth to it.

Yesterday when I was at market, Brahm suddenly appeared in my path.

Twenty-Sixth day of July

Yesterday when I was at market, Brahm suddenly appeared in my path. He told me I was pretty, even if I was a Jewess. He tried to touch me and again tried to take me to his room at the tavern. I took his hand off of my arm and walked away. As I walked off he called after me. "I know what your uncle the wizard has been doing and so does the one true holy church!"

I stopped. "What do you think he is doing?"

Brahm again came close to me, too close, and I felt his stinking breath on me. "Oh, perhaps I haven't told them yet, but I easily could! I have heard about these 'alchemists' and I know that to cast their spells they must light their rooms with special candles made from special tallow, tallow rendered from the fat of *Christian babies*!"

I thought I would become sick. What a horrid suggestion! If Brahm told such an awful lie to the bishop, our lives and the lives of every Jew in Grotinion would be destroyed!

"Oh, how bishop Michael would enjoy to hear such tales! He is highly favored for the papal throne and destroying a Jew wizard would only enhance his reputation. *Possibly* I would be less likely to believe, or more importantly, have to *tell* such a story if I knew you were a *friend*." I had seen him leer at the tavern trollops the way he now looked at me. God help me, I promised to meet him come the next market day and I headed for home as swiftly as I could.

The golem was almost finished when I arrived home. Two of Master Borah's slaves were busy polishing its surface. Master Borah and Uncle were in an animated conversation about which angel should be invoked to breathe spirit into the golem. The slaves babbled at one another in Lingua Franca too quickly for me to understand. I was fatigued and went to bed.

Twenty-Seventh day of July

I awoke this morning to find that the house was empty. I went up to the tower workroom to see if Uncle was about, but found only two of Master Borah's slaves cleaning up dust and stone chips from around the great statue. I saw that on the statue's forehead was now the name of the angel URIEL written in Enochian characters sketched out in graphite. One of the slaves spoke enough Greek to tell me that Master Borah and Uncle Raveh had gone to town to obtain some special herbs. I was troubled, for I had yet to tell Uncle of my conversation with Brahm. Adding to my anxiety, the homunculus was incessantly tapping with its one tiny hoof as it always did. While the tapping wasn't terribly loud, it echoed throughout the tower and set my nerves on edge. I had taken to calling the nasty little thing "Knock" after this annoying habit. Uncle says that the useless little imp doesn't deserve so fine a name and that I should call it after its other distinctive habit of flinging its own dung at everything and everyone.

21ˢᵀ CENTURY

A good portion of the scroll had been completely worm eaten and almost a hundred lines were totally indecipherable. Offenberg was not all that bothered by this because he believed that gaps in the story could be filled in from the Enochian scroll. It took him only a short time to discover the relevant passages in the notes of Ravinius Magnus.

CHAPTER 4

All of the preparations and invocations had been performed. All that remained was to inscribe the name and the creature would be born. I felt that I needed to obtain oil of rosemary to anoint the golem to help balance it against malign forces and took Borah to town with me so that the smith might regrind his chisels. It would be a terrible thing if the stone should crack or split when the name of the angelic force was inscribed. I had selected the archangel Uriel as the source of the creature's life for he was the bringer of wisdom *and* the master of thunder and power.

Both Borah and I performed our chores without incident and were preparing to return home when I noticed a few men gathered outside of the tavern who scrutinized Borah and me as we directed the slaves loading the wagon. When they saw me return their gaze they all made the sign of the cross, one of them mouthing the words "Jew bastard" and quickly re-entered the tavern. While I have never been closely associated with the Christian community save for those necessities that were required by law and to do business, neither had I ever been given reason to fear or be feared by them. Our Christian emperor had explicitly extended to the Jews the right to live at peace within the empire, so why the reaction of these men?

I found out when I arrived home and spoke with my niece. Little Jemma was so afraid of what this Brahm fellow might say and when I heard what slander he had threatened, I was both angered and saddened. I picked up a mallet and one of Borah's chisels and stepped up on the ladder before the golem. With the sleeve of my robe I rubbed away the graphite name of the angel. I placed the chisel against the statue's forehead.

Borah called out, "Think, dear friend, for once you have done this thing, it is truly writ in stone!"

I hesitated but a heartbeat, but that is all it took for Brahm's slander to again surface in my mind. I carefully cut letters in Hebrew, the language of the most holy Torah. I invoked this new being to serve a different power, not an angel but an idea, TRUTH. I carved the word אמת, *emet*, truth. I made the letters carefully, and though I am not the master stone cutter that Borah is, **_GOD_** guided my hand as I labored to make the lettering bold and clear. I was

"… it took me a few seconds to notice that the eyes of the statue were now examining me."

so concentrated on making the conformation of the letters perfect that it took me a few seconds to notice that the eyes of the statue were now examining me. Borah had sculpted the golem with closed eyes but now the eyes were opened, twin orbs of milky crystal that shaded to transparency at the pupils. I stepped back and those eyes tracked to follow my every move. Jemma gave a startled little cry and Borah clasped my shoulder in our shared triumph. "Jesus Christ, most holy," he said under his breath. The homunculus laughed mockingly from his cage. The eyes of the golem tracked about the room. They sounded like millstones as they shifted in their sockets.

It was essential for me to keep my composure. I spoke to the creature and prayed that my voice would not waver too much. "I am your creator and master! You will obey me in all things. Do you understand what I have said?"

The creature nodded its massive head slowly.

"Step forward and kneel before me!"

The golem stepped forward, knocking over and then stepping on and break-

"Jemma has a special fascination with the powerful creation."

ing, the ladder that had still leaned against its chest. It knelt before me on one knee with bowed head. Even kneeling, it was quite a bit taller than I.

"You are the golem, your name is TRUTH because you live to destroy lies."

Unlike the homunculus, the golem proved to be an excellent servant. It transported water from the well and would carry even very large stones for a field wall with no effort at all. Indeed, the golem never revealed any limit to his strength. I wondered if *he* might be mighty enough to tear down the Pyramids.

In his idle hours, I commanded the golem to sit on a stone bench in the tower workshop.

Jemma has a special fascination with the powerful creation and has taken upon herself the task of teaching it about the world. They are both innocents, but she is small and weak and the golem is great and mighty.

21ˢᵀ CENTURY

Ronald shook his head as he read the professor's translation. "Obviously, this is some sort of symbolic tale, like so many alchemical documents."

Offenberg was subdued in his response. "So it would seem. When we have completely translated both documents, we'll have a better idea. I'm working on another section of the girl's diary. That will tell us more."

CHAPTER 5

Third day of August

I decided to try and teach the golem to read. I think he may have already known how to somehow, for he picked it up very quickly, or so it seems for his eyes track the words on the page. He must be very smart, but it is so hard to tell as his face bears almost no expression whatsoever. I know not what he thinks, whether he is happy or sad.

He cannot speak at all so I tried to get him to write. His hand is too big and too strong to hold a quill or a stylus and his great fingers simply tore through a sheet of vellum when he picked it up.

"How can you communicate with me?" I asked.

The golem placed his huge hand on the stone sill of the tower room window and closed his eyes for a few seconds. To my amazement, when he removed his hand from the sill, there were raised letters in the stone as if it had flowed to form them at the golem's will. The words read, *truth is silent*.

I don't know what he meant. When he wrote "truth" did he mean his own name? If so, it was indeed a true statement, but if he did not then I dearly hope he is mistaken. He did not perform the trick again that day, but I told Uncle Raveh about it and he seemed very intrigued.

Over some days the words of the golem have become more frequent. I asked him if he had feelings. On one of the stones of the field wall he made the words *truth knows of anger pity faith love. truth yet knows them not and needs them not. truth is the earth.* It was like the pronouncements of the ancient oracle at Delphi before the bishops had her temple destroyed. Had the creature said that in spite of the fact that it was aware of the existence of these emotions, it could not, nor did it need to experience them itself? When it said it *was* the Earth, did it mean that the Earth was without love or anger or pity? I wonder if, unlike man, the golem cannot feel the love of God. Does he not in the truest sense have a heart of stone? I knew there was meaning, perhaps profound meaning there, but only a philosopher could properly interpret the words.

On another occasion I asked him what being suddenly brought to life was like. Upon a stone of the tower wall it made the words, *begin- the word -then light.* Had he paraphrased the opening of the Torah? Over a time, many stones around the property have become marked with lines from the golem. They are always in peculiar phrasings. The golem doesn't think like a man, the golem thinks like the golem.

21ST CENTURY

Members of Offenberg's team had been puzzled by broken bits of stone with raised lettering in Hebrew. The content of the writing didn't seem to convey much, but the method of their carving was odd and had been noted for further investigation. Offenberg had not thought them to be related to the great stone hand at first. Now he was feeling a need to revise that notion. There was the beginning of an explanation in the Enochian scroll which the archaeologists now commonly referred to as the "Ravinius text."

CHAPTER 6

Jemma has given herself much entertainment having taught the golem to make words on stone surfaces. It surprises me not that it should have this ability for the creature being entirely of the element of Earth can affect all things of the earth for that is its elemental affinity. The dear girl is deluded in thinking that the golem's words have any meaning, though. She has showed it many scrolls and it has seen words, but cannot comprehend and reproduces them as a man would draw a picture. This creature has not the will of a man nor the desires nor the feelings of a man. It moves as I have commanded it to move and if I command it not to move then it shall remain inert until I call upon it to move once more.

My Friend Borah said he must take his leave. He has seen proof enough that the stone of **_GOD'S_** forge indeed can have remarkable properties and will sell the rest for use in making carvings for the cathedral at Constantinople. Jemma and I saw him and his wagons off after the golem did all the loading. The slaves grumbled a bit about their jobs being taken over by an infernal device. Borah laughed heartily at their gripes. "*You had best hope that I not make one of these creatures for myself! I would sell you all off to work on some dull farm rather than see the world as a servant of Borah. Enjoy your afternoon of idleness, for there shall be work aplenty for you on the morrow.*" The wagons headed off to the east and I returned to my studies.

As I write, the golem is putting up a new shelf in my workroom for books and glassware. He builds them from stone that he molds with his hands the way a potter might mold wet clay. Even if I had a method of applying as much force as the creature's hands can command, the stone would break and crumble, but beneath the hand of the golem, it flows like mud. Similarly, the golem can repair itself. It shattered a finger moving a stone a day ago. It retrieved the pieces and held them to their original spot and the parts rejoined so perfectly that no defect could be seen there afterward. I believe that so long as the *word* remains writ upon its brow, the golem shall walk the Earth for only that erasure can permanently destroy him.

I know that I charged the golem with the protection of my household in my anger at Brahm's slander, but I have kept the creature too busy to perform that task.

My niece vanished this morning! Truly I fear she is the victim of some villainy. I found the Mogen David star she wore around her neck lying on the ground by the well. How am I to find her? Jemma is the light of my life and has brought joy to my old age, I cannot allow her to be taken from me.

I have had a thought. The golem is of the Earth, in reality, it *is* the Earth! The golem can find Jemma, retrieve her and return her to her home. I called out and ordered the golem into my presence and I held up the Mogen David star before his expressionless face.

"Jemma is gone!" I declared.

For the first time, I observed a hint of expression in the creature's face. It had a look of interest.

"She has been taken by a

"The dear girl is deluded in thinking that the golem's words have any meaning."

*"For the first time, I observed a hint of expression
in the creature's face. It had a look of interest."*

villain. The spreader of lies."

The golem somehow looked thoughtful. One great hand reached up and touched the word upon its brow. It scowled. I was taken aback. It touched the stone wall and the words ***only truth abides*** appeared on the stone.

I told it, "You are part of the Earth and the Earth knows all things! You already possess the knowledge needed to find her! Go forth! Go forth and leave not one stone upon another until you have found her! Let nothing deter you! No life is more precious than hers!" In that moment when I allowed my dismay and anger to control me, I unleashed that mighty force upon the unwitting world.

The creature reached out and took from me the pendant and placed it in the

"Go forth! Go forth and leave not one stone upon another until you have found her!"

palm of its hand. The star sunk into the stone as if it were quicksand and then the surface was again whole and solid. For a moment, it stood in place and vibrated. I suspect that it was feeling the resonance of the Earth itself. It then walked from the room and thence from the tower and toward the town. I called after it, "Return my beloved niece, my Jemma!" It touched the garden wall and the words *jemma above all things* were left there as it marched away.

Now it is several hours later and I know not what transpires in the town and I have great fear of what I may discover if I go there, but go there I must!

21ST CENTURY

Even putting together the two accounts, the narrative as expressed in the scrolls of Ravinius Magnus and his niece Jemma, has a major gap at this point. Professor Offenberg was frustrated to be so close to assembling the entire tale and yet finding crucial parts missing. Weeks went by as the scrolls were carefully examined.

It was the yet poorly understood grimoire that ended up providing the answer. At one point in the collection of texts there were a plethora of cipher tables that unraveled some of the obscure languages that Ravinius Magnus had used to record his formulae. One of them was a comparison with a language known previously in only one other document, the so-called "Williamsburg Codex." This book turned up in the hands of a New York rare book dealer in 1912 and had since become recognized as one of the more baffling artifacts from medieval times. The language of its composition was completely unknown. It was lavishly illustrated with pictures seemingly illustrative to alchemy, art, geography and erotica. For this mysterious volume, the grimoire of Ravinius Magnus was a Rosetta Stone.

The Williamsburg Codex was the work of Alexandrios Boraion, sculptor, traveler, scientist and scholar, previously unknown to history. Passages from the book reveal that he was the stonecutter "Borah" identified in the scrolls of Ravinius Magnus. Here is what has thus far been translated of the relevant passages.

Chapter 7

Indeed, the statue that was given life by the Jewish alchemist Ravinius was one of the strangest, and ultimately both wondrous and tragic, of my accomplishments and, it turned out, not one that I could merely leave behind. After some days' ride to the south, I felt the Holy Spirit ignite a voice within my mind. Something was unfinished and there were events that I must witness.

I returned to Grotinion seven days after I had taken my leave. Constantine had sent word that another sculptor had come less dear for the decoration of his new basilica. They call this emperor Copronymus, "shit named," because as a babe he shat in his own baptismal font, just as now he shits upon great artists! The loss of the contract was probably God telling me that my return to Grotinion was more important. It could only be the power of almighty God that could inspire such a lack of taste in so great an emperor. I resolved to return to the house of Ravinius and once events were dealt with there, I would go to Alexandria where a tomb for the governor was being built. Perhaps I will be magnanimous enough to offer my services there.

Before I could even reach the house of Ravinius, evidence that something was terribly wrong presented itself.

The golem was in the square of the town. I could imagine no circumstance under which Ravinius would permit such a thing! The creature slowly walked. It moved carefully in the street, holding its huge hands over the ground like it was dowsing. Here and there it would pause and beneath one hand or the other ripples would pass through the ground, through the very cobbles of the street as if the earth were water in which a pebble had been dropped.

I called to my slaves to halt the wagons. I didn't want the creature to pay me undue heed. The slaves and I dismounted and followed the creature at a safe distance. I prayed to holy Jesus to guide my actions for the aura of impending calamity hung over these events.

Suddenly the golem turned with a speed that I would not have expected. In truth, the creature of living stone had moved not so very much more quickly than a hesitating, somewhat jerky march. Now it had almost cat-like reactions. It trotted toward a stone-walled structure that I believe housed the

"Stopping before one wall it struck it with a mighty blow."

village tavern. Stopping before one wall it struck it with a mighty blow. A cloud of powdered mortar puffed out, but the stones held their position. Not so for the golem's second blow. The wall came down and the golem started pushing stones aside to get into the house. A small knot of men piled out of the door and scattered through the square. One of them spotted me and ran in my direction. As he got closer, I could hear that he was babbling in Gothic. My slave, Horzdt, told me that he said that the monster had looked right at him and was begging me to save him. He said that he was Brahm, a soldier of the Imperial legion and would

"The golem emerged from the hole in the wall holding a tiny and frail looking girl."

see that I was rewarded. I was skeptical. This man had more the appearance of a villain than a disciplined soldier. He also had blood on his hands.

The golem emerged from the hole in the wall holding a tiny and frail looking girl covered in welts and bruises, her tunica torn in tatters leaving her barely covered, blood running from her mouth and nose. To my horror, I realized that this was Jemma, the innocent and beautiful niece of Ravinius Magnus, and I was sure that she was dead. The eyes of the golem seemed to have a subtle glow that I found frightening, but this Brahm fellow found it even more so. He seized my garment and screamed "It will kill me! It will kill me!" In the Gothic tongue, he called upon Jesus and then also upon the more ancient deities that the Goths once served. The golem approached our group holding the broken body of the child. Its stone lips curled back to reveal smooth teeth that were never carved by my hand. In giving this creature life, its animating spirit supplied it with all of those details seemingly just to show me what a poor artist I am compared with the architect of all life. Its mouth opened in a silent roar of rage. Brahm shook as he stood in place, his legs would not move even as the golem approached more closely. It stopped before him and knelt down to bring its eyes level with his. It laid Jemma's battered body ever so gently upon the ground. It took such care even though she seemed to be far beyond all pain. The golem placed a hand on the cobbles and pulled it back. The word **murderer** was embossed upon the stone. I don't think this Brahm fellow could read, but I'm certain that the accusation was clear. As the Goth wailed pathetically, the golem reached out with a single great stone hand and enclosed his entire head. It stood lifting him as he kicked and flailed his arms. The rest of us looked upward and backed away. The eyes of the golem glowed brighter for an instant as it tightened the hand that held Brahm into a fist and gore squirted horribly from between the stone fingers. The Goth's body twitched once then hung limp. The golem dropped him and stooped to pick up the body of the girl. I called to the golem "Stop!" and it did and then turned. It walked quickly up to my heavy wagon and tore away the tarp. There I had other blocks of stone from God's Forge. It placed its hand upon one.

to you I owe no obedience

"I made you!" I cried. "I built your body!"

The creature silently regarded me. Was that *contempt* writ upon its nigh immobile features? As if *I* could create a living being or even Ravinius Magnus! No, I had made a vessel to be filled and Raveh had merely invited life in, but the power to create it remained, now and always, in the hands of God. I realize now, that I had committed blasphemy with those words, but, Blessed Jesus help me, I could not prevent myself from going on. "You are a monster, you have no soul!"

The golem's eyes grew wide and I feared that it might now kill me as it had killed the Goth. It pointed to the inert figure of the girl on the ground.

"The girl? What of her?"

The stone giant laid a hand on the stone. *her life was my soul*

In the name of the Holy Saints! The creature believed that the girl had been the source of its own soul! What would happen now that its soul was dead?

"What are you without her life?"

The golem again bared its teeth and struck the block of stone a blow with its clenched fist that both pulverized the entire block and broke the back of my strongest wagon as if it had been a mere splinter. The horses panicked and started rearing and kicking. The stone giant attacked them throwing them this way and that. A horse was tossed at and brought down a cottage where it lay broken and dying

"… the golem reached out with a single great stone hand and enclosed his entire head."

another landed in the branches of a tree from which it would eventually fall and be killed. I quickly ordered the slaves to cut the others loose. Chen, who had been my faithful teamster, was struck by the fist of the golem and killed instantly as he tried to save the horses. The golem now stalked about the town square, breaking whatever came in its reach.

While its attention was diverted, I went over to the body of the girl and laid my hand on her chest to see if the pulse of life was still evident. I praised the almighty Lord when I felt the beating of her heart. I looked up just in time to see that the golem had noticed me. I had to at first back away and then run away as the golem broke into a trot. Each of the monster's steps spanned five yards so it took it little time to cover much distance. From the edge of the square I saw the creature pick up Jemma ever so tenderly. This carven parody of humanity was more gentle with her than a mother with a newborn. That those huge hands of stone could be capable of such soft, dare I say it, *loving*, tenderness! This creature could move from destroyer to preserver in the blink of an eye.

I realized that Raveh must be completely ignorant of the fact that the golem was laying waste to the entire town! I called to my remaining slaves to round up a horse for me and in short order, my quarryman Hamid led the calmest mare to me. I mounted her and ordered them to not lose sight of the golem or the girl, then I turned and galloped off toward the house of Ravinius.

"'Twas on the road that I encountered the alchemist. He was in an unfortunate state. Standing directly in front of him saying his name, I could scarce get his attention.

"Raveh! Raveh, my friend! Ravinius Magnus!" He blinked and finally focused. "Borah!"

"Yes, it is I, old friend. What has happened?"

He told the whole tale alternately weeping and shouting, of how Jemma had been taken by a local man, a thief and rascal, and how he had called upon the golem to rescue her. He had ordered the thing to kill if necessary to bring her safely home.

Raveh's eyes widened as he looked past me for a moment. I turned to see the golem resolutely marching up the road with the girl cradled in its arms followed at a distance by my single remaining wagon and only three of my slaves. Apparently Kuba, the blackamoor, had also been killed by the golem, for his and Chen's

אמת

"The creature's eyes still had the strange red glow…"

battered bodies were laid in the wagon. Only sweet Jesus knew how many of the townsfolk had become the victims of the creature's aimless wrath. I prayed that most had taken the chance to run when they could. The creature's eyes still had the strange red glow, a little like coals in a fire but much more like the molten stone that flows from a volcanic crater.

Raveh stepped away from me and stood directly in the golem's way. "Stop," he said.

I wondered if it would, for it continued to advance until it was very nearly toe to toe with Raveh. It halted and looked down. Ravinius Magnus met its eyes as evenly as he could manage. "Give me the girl."

The golem hesitated.

"Give me the girl!"

The golem's will to obey overcame its obstinacy and it laid Jemma's body in Raveh's outstretched arms. He hugged her to his heart and allowed himself to weep for only a few seconds. Gaining control, he brought the girl over to me and begged me to take her. Again I checked her heartbeat and it was still strong, Raveh must surely have felt it also. I took her and laid her on a bed of straw in the wagon.

Raveh held the golem's eyes. "Follow me." He turned and walked back up the road. The golem followed slowly. I and the wagon also followed taking care to maintain a distance from the golem. In a short time we came to the tower.

I approached Raveh. "Will Jemma live?," he asked.

"I believe so, she is hurt, but she is young and will recover. What of the golem? What are you going to do, my friend?," I asked.

"I don't know. How many has it harmed?"

"Too many. At least three townsmen are dead and two of my slaves, Brahm the Goth most gruesomely."

Ravinius almost started to weep again. "It must be destroyed, Borah. It must be returned to lifeless stone."

I paused before I spoke again. I was unsure of my knowledge, but the alchemist had to know all. "I have spoken to it. I believe it may have a soul. If this is true, then it would be a sin to kill it…murder."

"Now that this has happened, it is only a matter of time before the people of the town come to murder *me*. What if that happens and this thing still walks the Earth? I must regardless of it possessing a soul or not and God shall decide the consequence!" With that Ravinius turned and walked over to the golem. "Go into the tower." He said.

The alchemist and the stone giant both entered the tower. I followed a few paces behind, for my curiosity had overcome my natural prudence. Slowly we walked up the spiral of stone stairs that led to the laboratory of Ravinius Magnus. Outside a storm gathered ominously and there was the aura of grim portent in the air. In the work room, Ravinius commanded the golem to go and stand upon the spot where it had been created, where it had been hewn from stone by my own hands.

A bat flapped in through the window, an ordinary enough event, but this night it seemed full of evil portent, reminding me of the legend of God's Forge. It circled the room once, making the homunculus cackle with glee, and was gone, but the dark foreboding remained.

The homunculus laughed mockingly from its cage, not at the golem, but at Ravinius. The golem's eyes again reddened and I feared that Raveh might become the focus of its violence. I was wrong for it reached out a great stone hand and plucked the cage that held the homunculus from the hook from which it had been suspended and brought close to its face. The eyes of the golem met those of the homunculus and the tiny creature had one of its rare moments of silence. The golem seemed to recognize the little man as similar to itself in being but a poor imitation of almighty God's work. The silence of the homunculus lasted but a few seconds and then it pointed a mocking finger at the golem and let forth with peals of impish laughter. Only the smallest squeak was heard from the little imp as the golem closed its hand, crushing the cage and homunculus as one and then rolled it between its great hands until it was but a small ball of gore and metal. It tossed it on the floor where it rolled between the alchemist's feet.

"You see!," cried Ravinius, "You are an instrument of destruction!"

The golem touched the stone wall. ***truth is your instrument this you have said***

Raveh squinted at the lettering. For the first time, I believe, he seemed to understand that the words of the golem actually had relevant meaning. Slowly he said, "Yes, you are my instrument. I created you to do my bidding." The alchemist suddenly stopped speaking. He realized what he had done, that he had told the golem to let nothing deter it. Raveh stepped back. I could see the doubt in his face. How could he have done this thing?

"I must destroy you and give myself to prayer."

The golem again touched the wall. This time the letters were somewhat larger.

thou shalt not kill

"I shouldn't kill as you have done? Besides, you are not alive! You cannot love or hate or feel remorse. You are an automaton! Through you, I have killed already!"

jemma above all things

Raveh committed many sins in this questionable enterprise, but I think this gravest, because he clearly knew that what he was about to say was untrue. "Then why did you let her die?"

Beside me I heard a child's tiny gasp.

21ST CENTURY

The remainder of the diary of the girl Jemma was not organized by date and most likely written all at once at a later time. How much later, we have yet to determine.

CHAPTER 8

Only now can I speak of that day. The things that happened are both wondrous and horrifying.

I was drawing water for the midday meal for Uncle when I was seized from behind with a hand placed firmly over my mouth! A bag was drawn over my head and my wrists and ankles were swiftly and expertly bound and I was roughly thrown in the back of a wagon that carried me off with great speed and much painful bumping. I was brought into a building that I believed to be the village tavern based on what I smelt. I heard one drunken voice call out, "Oh-ho, and what new prize has Brahm brought home?"

Brahm, 'twas he, of course! "A ripe young Jewess who will become my concubine!"

I was then in a quieter, but even smellier place and the bag was pulled off of my head. There he was with his leering face and his stinking breath: Brahm. He leaned forward and tried to kiss me. I turned my head away in disgust. He slapped me and said, "That is a warning! You belong to me now and will do as pleases me!" He tried to kiss me again and again I turned away and again he slapped me only much harder this time. I cried out, "What do you want of me? Why are you hurting me?"

"Little whore! Don't you want a real man?"

My heart was racing from fear and it races now as I recall it. "I have no knowledge of men and why should I wish to gain it from a man that hurts me?!?" He struck me again and then again and again and soon I was no longer even there.

I hurt all over when I awoke and rain fell upon my face, pleasant and cool. I was no longer at the tavern or even in the town. Looking upward I saw the tower of Uncle Raveh. Painfully, I rolled onto my side to find myself face to face with a dead man. It was Chen, slave of Master Borah. His neck was twisted and broken and one side of his head was flat. Blood trickled from his ear. His dead eyes stared in different directions. 'Twas an awful sight.

With great care I raised myself up on my elbows and then I saw Kuba. Sweet Kuba who has sung such wonderful songs and told such merry stories! The sight of him stiffened me with horror for his body was in two pieces. I wanted to cry out at the gruesome sight of the two dead slaves, but somehow I could not. My heart was racing and I hurt all over, I knew not if I could even stand, but somehow I knew that I must try. I could see that I was in one of Master Borah's wagons. Somehow I brought myself to crawl over the two bodies and got down from the wagon. It felt as if my legs would fold beneath me, but I remained standing, if only unsurely. The rain refreshed me and I started to walk to the tower. I made my way up the seemingly endless stairs although I had to stop several times to catch my breath and let the pain subside. Finally I reached the doorway of Uncle's laboratory where stood Master Borah with his back to me. As quietly as I could, I went over to stand beside him. If he even knew I was there, he paid me no heed, for he was enthralled by what transpired in the work room.

We stood in the shadows as the golem inscribed words on the wall. It wrote

jemma above all things

Uncle said "Then why did you let her die?"

I gasped! He was going to let the golem think I was dead! I was going to cry out that I was not dead when Master Borah covered my mouth with his hand and held me tight. "Keep your peace, girl. This is how it must be!" He whispered. I struggled briefly, but I had not the strength.

The golem looked at Uncle Raveh and there was genuine pain etched on its great stone face. It staggered and steadied itself with a hand against the wall. I would never have believed that the golem was capable of such anguish

"You failed. You are useless!"

I was stricken by what Uncle was doing! I had to say something. I tried to struggle against Master Borah's grip.

The golem with sudden speed reached out and seized Uncle Raveh's wrist. Its hand was so large that it enclosed his arm almost from wrist to elbow. It placed its other hand upon the wall. ***truth dies*** The golem pulled Raveh toward him and lifted uncle's captive hand to his brow. This left Uncle Raveh stretched as high as he could reach, barely standing on his toes.

"My Lord!" he prayed, "My Lord, what will be my reward for striving to create as you have?" His anguish was real, but I now understood what he somehow could not. One does not honor God by attempting to take his place. Heaven answered his prayer with a powerful bolt of lightning that struck the highest point on the tower. The power of that bolt of lightning seemed to seek out the golem and Uncle Raveh while leaving Master Borah and myself untouched. The golem stood still while Raveh's body jerked and convulsed most horribly. I could not look away nor could I even shut my eyes. The golem and Raveh were enclosed in an aura that could only be described as angelic light. Uncle's hand seemed now to be made of a living vapor that flashed with tiny lightning bolts and then swiftly became pure flame. Another second and it was swirling water and then it was the same stone as the golem. The golem lowered his hand, allowing uncle to stand flat on his feet but did not release him. The flesh of his hand was restored to its normal state.

On the golem's forehead, the letter א was gone from the word אמת (*emet*), *truth*, making it מת (*met*), *dead*. Uncle Raveh shook and cried out, this time inarticulately.

I broke free of Borah's grip, ran into the light and cried out to the golem, "No! Please don't! Don't die!" It was too late. I met its eyes as the light of life disappeared from them. Suddenly, lightning again struck the tower with an ear shattering blast and the floor started to move as if all the stones were now loose. Borah leapt forward and picked me up, dragging me toward the stairs.

The golem stood there, now as dead as any other lump of stone, tottering back and forth. Raveh looked at his arm and realized that he was still gripped by the creature, the huge stone hand never to open again. He looked up and screamed as the golem fell over right through the crumbling wall, dragging him helplessly to inevitable destruction.

Carrying me, Master Borah plunged down the stone staircase as the dust of the crumbling tower chased us. We were followed out the door by a huge fountain of dust that coated us both from head to toe. Master Borah threw me down in the mud and covered my body with his. We turned just in time to see the last part of the tower fall to the earth.

"He looked up and screamed as the golem fell over right through the crumbling wall, dragging him helplessly to inevitable destruction."

What had been the tower was now but a pile of loose stones in the rain. The storm started to clear almost as quickly as it had come up and the stars came out in their full splendor. Borah and I sat there in the mud until two of the slaves came and helped us up.

Around that time a group of men from the village showed up with torches and farming tools. They apparently had it in mind to destroy the golem and kill uncle Raveh. I told them that they both were already dead and that they were lucky in that, for they would never have been able to destroy the golem. The villager who questioned me, a blacksmith named Kyril, didn't hear the answer he wanted to and made a move to strike me but Borah stepped between him and me. Even though the sculptor was a head shorter than him, Kyril was reluctant to attempt to move Master Borah. The mob contented itself with burning the house and barn and two monks set a stake with an icon of saint Demetrios upon the rubble of the tower. They had all left within an hour.

Master Borah's slaves turned over stone after stone until they uncovered the battered body of Uncle Raveh amongst the broken pieces of the golem. I located the Book of Psalms and read passages from it when we buried him along with Master Borah's good and faithful slaves. How I had loved Uncle Raveh and how wrong he had been in his quest to understand life. That secret lies not in the mechanics of the flesh but in the mystery of the soul. I pray that almighty God will understand that it was an error born of devotion and that it not cost him his place at the feet of the Lord.

Master Borah took me under his wing and I became the manager of his caravan in charge of the horses, slaves and wagons. My first job is to purchase two new wagons. That has to be done in the south because after the golem's rampage in Grotinion, bishop Michael decreed that all Jews had to move out of the diocese. Had Uncle Raveh not been killed, there is no doubt that the bishop would have ordered him tortured and executed. We are going to Alexandria, but before we go, I will bury at the site of the tower the grimoire and notebook of Uncle Raveh and this diary as well as a piece of the golem. That poor tortured creature, that servant of truth, deserved a decent burial and the account of how it was given life is best hidden from the eyes of man for all time.

21ST CENTURY

Offenberg now had a preliminary translation of the scrolls and all that was left for him to do until he could return to the dig next season was to carefully examine the great stone hand. It was fine-grained Jurassic limestone that probably had originated somewhere in Northern Europe. One of the geologists at the University would be able to pin that down for him. In the meanwhile, he wanted to take it in for chemical analysis to see if the surface had ever been painted. He stumbled as he strained to lift it onto a cart and it fell to the concrete floor reaking into two pieces. As he looked down in dismay he saw something glint in the sunlight that streamed in the window. Protruding from the stone was a bit of silver. He looked more closely. It was still half imbedded in the stone as if it had been part of it, but there was no doubt of what it was, a silver Mogen David star.

"Protruding from the stone was a bit of silver."

THE END

Unlikely

It was a good job. The place was called Crandall Labs; I had no idea what precisely they did, but it was "big" science and they had a lot of government contracts. The job came to me via a reference from an old buddy, the guy who previously held it. I rarely saw my boss, I was mostly left to myself and the money was pretty good. The hours were the exact opposite of the ones I had been keeping at my last job. Eight PM to six AM, the night shift. Peaceful. A whole different pace.

My job was simple to the point of absurdity, I merely had to monitor the network and make sure that any new files that came into the server were in the right folders so the techs could find them in the morning. This took up about two minutes once an hour or so.

Hours

By Seth Kallen Deitch

Art By Kim Deitch

The rest of my time was spent drinking coffee, shooting the bull with Bob, the downstairs security guard, or posting to Usenet about details of my admiration for pulp author Johnston McCulley.

When I went out to smoke or to the all-night market in the strip mall next door, I would surprise rats that hung near the back door dumpster. They would skitter into the shadows silently when they heard me step out, then observe me from the obscurity with eyes of a black just a tiny bit shinier than the black that enveloped them. There was an owl in the neighborhood who controlled their numbers, and presumably made their lives exciting. The rats always seemed like they were up to something. Something besides eating garbage, I mean. They looked sneaky.

The coffee from the convenience store had that "been in the pot too long" flavor. Hot, metallic, even when it was freshly brewed. I have no idea how they did it and asking would do me no good. The clerk was a generic brown-skinned man with a generic brown-skinned man accent that gave me no clue to his national origin. Most of humanity is some shade of brown. This fellow sort of pretended to understand English, but all he really ever said was "Yes, very good!" or tell me how much I owed. The radio behind the counter constantly emitted some sort of eastern sounding pop music, reedy, wailing. It was a faraway sound that added to the night's edgy ambience.

Once in a while there was a brown-skinned boy, about six years old, thin and delicate looking in a stained Pikachu T-shirt, who wandered about the store. I wondered what a child his age was doing up so late. He must be nocturnal like me. I once saw him making a fort of plastic milk crates out by the dumpster. He only spoke Hindustani or Quechua or Malay or whatever the hell it was, but that was only when he spoke at all. Mostly he just gazed inquiringly with large brown eyes. His expression was at odds with the unalloyed positivity of the cartoon character on his chest.

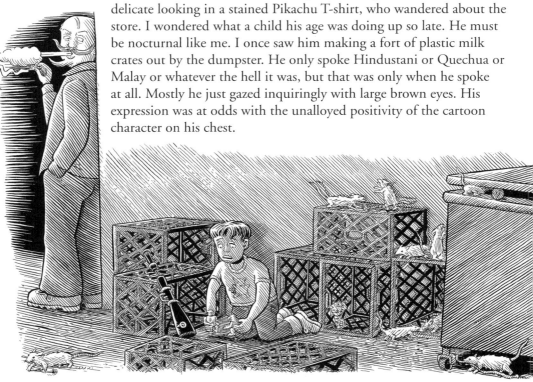

He and Pikachu inhabited different universes.

One time I bought a hot dog there and sat on the back stoop to eat it. A rat watched me speculatively from under the dumpster. On a whim, I broke the end off the frank and tossed it to him. He emerged from his shelter, his beady eyes scanning me with suspicion, and sniffed the morsel. The small rodent grunted and turned his back on the meat, sweeping it aside with his naked tail. I tossed the rest of the dog in the dumpster. If a rat won't eat it, I probably shouldn't either.

These were weird rats anyway. I would often step out the back to find them standing in a row or a circle, or walking in a line. Once I saw three of them stripping insulation from the

wires  of a discarded toaster with their sharp incisors. They broke off bits of the shiny wire and were carrying them away to God-knows-where. They scattered when they saw me.

Other odd things went on. From time to time I would hear a weird, cartoony voice reciting passages from *Moby-Dick*. Probably just some stupid screen saver, but it would catch me by surprise from time to time and give me a major case of the willies.

The nights blended into one another and I barely saw any of my friends or family. To them I was this ghost who sent them e-mails and left notes on the refrigerator. I rose at seven PM, even on weekends. By the time I was really ready to go out and do things, most of my friends were either in bed or working on their last drink. My weekend nights were mostly spent working on my novel *The New Adventures of the Son of Zorro*, and watching late movies. The novel occupied much of my time at work as well.

In this tale, Don Ricardo Vega (son of the original Zorro, whose story is told in Johnston McCulley's "The Curse of Capistrano" and several other pulp serials) is forced once more to don the mask of the legendary hero to protect the people from a deranged scientist with a mysterious airship who sought domination of the West.

High adventure, right? It added to the odd atmosphere of my job that my mind was in picturesque

old Spanish California while I was in twenty-first century Massachusetts on non-picturesque Route 128. As I worked on my book, I periodically printed out sections of the manuscript in progress to review and to show people. Copies kept disappearing. An overzealous janitor, I assumed.

On one Wednesday morning, I stopped in on my friend Jerry who generally was rising for his hard day of studied unemployment around the time I was arriving home from work. The guy makes a fine cup of Java and

is actually capable of having a semi-coherent conversation fresh out of bed, although the subject was usually whatever loony dream he had just been having. They mostly involved discovering arcane jazz records in strange places. He said that he frequently actually heard the content of these non-existent discs. I just assumed that he had some sort of connection to alternate dimensions and left it at that. He tended to agree.

"I was in a rooming house in Paducah, Kentucky, the place was run by a hunchback with a propeller beanie. It was an old Victorian. There was a beautifully carved organ in the parlor. On an end table next to it was a small cut glass dish of parlor beans. In my dream, I somehow knew that any Victorian parlor worthy of the name had a dish or two of these dry, rich brown beans sitting about. Of their

purpose, I can tell you nothing. The second day I was there, I noticed that the legs of all the furniture were replaced with stacks of old records. When the hunchback wasn't looking, I took down the end table and started looking at the titles.

"'*Bad Breaks and Bacon Grease*' by Eddie Fuller and his Collegiate Halfbacks.

"'*Dizzy Spells*' by the Bob Handle Five.

"'*Out of My Album*' by Olga Bibor and her Peasant Jazz Orchestra.

"'*Back Forty*' by the Jiving Jazz Farmers.

"'*Roll When You Walk*' by Curley Johnson.

"'*Two Cats in the Alley*' by Buddy Watson's Swinging Serenaders.

"'*Harlem Hijinks*' by Tall John Worrell.

"'*What's It To Ya'?*' by Johnny James and his Sioux City Syncopators.

"The hunchback caught me and warned me, 'Those are sinful sounds!'

Then I woke up."

"Are any of those records real?"
"Not in this universe."

I stirred my coffee even though I don't take anything in it.

"So, Jake", he asked me, "how much longer are you planning on keeping these unlikely hours?"

"I dunno, as long as it takes, I guess. The money's pretty good and I don't really have to do much."

"Uh-huh. So what goes on there?"

"I don't know what they actually do there. I have to keep an eye on some computers. I think the rats are up to something." I didn't know how odd it would sound until I actually said it out loud.

Jerry raised his eyebrows. "The *hell* you say! 'Up to something'? How do you mean?"

"They're acting sneaky."

"Isn't sneaky how rats act?"

"These ones act sneaky in unusual ways and when they see they are being watched, they start acting sneaky in the regular way."

"So you can tell the difference between 'regular' sneaky and 'unusual' sneaky?"

"When *you* say it, it sounds stupid."

"I have a feeling it would sound about the same coming out of anyone."

Jerry played me a few new 78rpm acquisitions and I went home to bed.

As the weeks wore on, the surreality of my situation seemed to fade somewhat. I got use to my largely solitary life, even grew to like it. I came, I kept an eye on things, I went home, I slept. Every

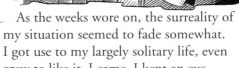

Friday, an interoffice envelope contained my paycheck. The brown-skinned man continued to dispense plastic wrapped nourishment, Bob the security guard continued to lie about all the women he slept with, the rats continued to scheme.

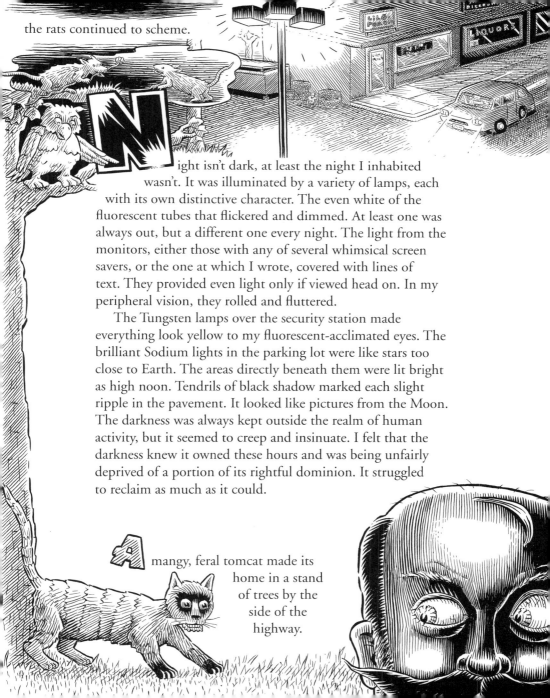

Night isn't dark, at least the night I inhabited wasn't. It was illuminated by a variety of lamps, each with its own distinctive character. The even white of the fluorescent tubes that flickered and dimmed. At least one was always out, but a different one every night. The light from the monitors, either those with any of several whimsical screen savers, or the one at which I wrote, covered with lines of text. They provided even light only if viewed head on. In my peripheral vision, they rolled and fluttered.

The Tungsten lamps over the security station made everything look yellow to my fluorescent-acclimated eyes. The brilliant Sodium lights in the parking lot were like stars too close to Earth. The areas directly beneath them were lit bright as high noon. Tendrils of black shadow marked each slight ripple in the pavement. It looked like pictures from the Moon. The darkness was always kept outside the realm of human activity, but it seemed to creep and insinuate. I felt that the darkness knew it owned these hours and was being unfairly deprived of a portion of its rightful dominion. It struggled to reclaim as much as it could.

A mangy, feral tomcat made its home in a stand of trees by the side of the highway.

Its genetic background must have been peculiar because it was mostly solid gray, but had tabby markings on its rump and hind legs and black paws. A raccoon mask adorned its face. I had never seen another cat with a similar coat. It haunted the convenience store dumpster and sometimes caught one of the rats. I saw this occur on one occasion. The stricken rat's fellows, instead of staying hidden, gathered to watch the cat carry away the twitching carcass, huddled, seemingly for mutual comfort.

They dispersed only when I came within six feet of the group.

I saw part of the victim on my way into work the next night by the side of the highway. I noticed that it was white rather than the generic brown or gray that rats usually were, its fur was just very soiled.

Jerry placed a cup of African roast in front of me.

"The rats are up to something. I know it."

"Again with the rats. You need another job. One where you have human beings to talk to."

"I don't *talk* to them. I have been *observing* them and they are **up to something**."

Jerry was taken aback by my intensity.

"Let me ask you…what would they want with copper wire? Do rats mourn their dead? They are keeping an eye on me."

"Shut up! You are freaking me out. Let the filthy rodents have their world and you get a fucking grip on yours." He smiled when he said it, but I got the impression that he really thought I might be wigging out a little.

I stopped mentioning the rats to Jerry after that morning. Our conversations returned to the usual subjects of old jazz, zeppelin technology and women. Old jazz was the constant standard, zeppelins were something I was researching for my book and women were what neither one of us had at the moment.

That night, I watched for an hour as one rat made trip after trip to the dumpster to retrieve only the cellophane wraps from packs of cigarettes. He made, like, thirty trips, just for cellophane.

When I was at the store, I asked the man about the rats.

"Let me ask you, sir, have you noticed anything unusual about the rats?"

"Yes, very good!"

"No, no, no. The **rats**. The ones that live by the dumpster."

He looked at me quizzically. "We don't have."

I rolled my eyes. "I'm not saying you are infested with them."

"No, not interested," he agreed.

"But, have you noticed the rats?"

"Eighty-nine cent each," he declared with absolute certainty.

"I don't want to buy them…ah, never mind, just ring me up for this." I placed a sixteen-ounce bottle of JOLT Cola and a pre-packaged egg-salad sandwich on the counter. He just stared at me.

"Um, don't you want money?"

"You don't want to buy!"

"I want the sandwich and the soda, I just don't want rats."

"Yes, very good! No rats!" He started merrily punching keys on the register. I have no idea what he thought our conversation had been about.

The air was hot, humid and still that night. The dumpsters exuded a rich, cadaver breath flavored putrescence. The smoke from my cigarette hung in the air congealed, as if it feared dissipation, the way a human fears death.

From across the parking lot I heard a tortured yowl. The cat had bolted from beneath Crandall's dumpster

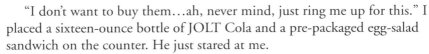

stopping every few feet to claw frantically at its face. As it came beneath one of the Sodium lights, I saw that its

furry mask was blood-streaked from a wounded eye. Beneath the dumpster were a dozen beady gloss-black reflections.

The cat rolled on the pavement beneath the lamp and finally dashed off to its woods. I walked up to the patch of light on the ground where the cat had paused. On the ground was a pencil with a blood-stained blade made from a part of an Aluminum soda can bound to it with multiple wraps of copper wire.

In spite of the hot night, I shivered.

I didn't see the cat for several nights. Just when I had assumed that he must be dead, he reappeared, gaunt and starving. He moved sluggishly on one side of his body. Evidently, the blade had touched his brain also. A loose lid now lay concave over the space of his ruined eye. The need for food had forced him to overcome his misery. For the rest of his life he would root through garbage for sustenance. With only one eye, his days as an effective hunter were over.

I couldn't do the same thing all the time. I would get blocked on the novel, I would become infuriated with some response I got on alt.fan.zorro (being called a "nerdy fanboy" by someone who admits, nay *brags*, that he wears a "Star Trek" uniform to weddings, is just *too* much), sometimes I would simply have had too much coffee. I started hacking into files on some of the work stations and found out about a handful of Crandall's projects. I'm not boasting, security on the files I found was pretty lax. It didn't take anything like an expert to find them. As often as not there was a link on the desktop. Or a folder labeled "Project files."

They had been working on a few things that were more or less boring and that I had unclear understanding of, stuff like wireless network cards. Useful, no doubt, but not too sexy. More interesting

was similar work on a version of the same thing that was actually implanted in a user's body that would allow him to communicate with a computer network without any other appliance. They had tested it with various animals. It allowed the test animals to remember how they performed tasks and compare their previous solutions with the current problem. They had made a mouse that could use its eyes for the computer to read books for the blind. They had studied the notion of using birds and bats for remote probes. Another experiment had used a parrot as a text-to-speech tool that was easier to understand and had more inflection than a synthesized voice. That explained *Moby-Dick*. The implant could be made cheaply compared to manufacturing a robot to perform the same task. Interesting. These gizmos could give even creatures with small brains, access to computer resources.

The reports claimed that the minds of the animals could effectively be enlarged to human levels with the computer network doing much of the actual data handling.

In the distance, from behind some closed laboratory door, a comically inhuman voice squawked "…ere now it has been related how Ahab was wont to pace his quarter-deck, taking regular turns at either limit…"

I now *officially* had the willies.

I dug up and printed out every paper on the subject I could find and put them in an envelope to take home and read in depth.

I was having a second cup of coffee and Jerry was still reading.

"I had no idea they could actually *do* this sort of thing," said Jerry.

"Neither did I. Do you suppose that the rats were worked on that way?"

"Come on!" He put the papers down. "You are obsessed with those rats!"

"They experiment on rats."

"They experiment on the cute white rats, not on gray sewer rats."

"The rats are really white, not gray. I saw one up close, he was just dirty, or…"

"Or what?"

"Or maybe they change the color of their fur on purpose. Disguise."

Jerry rolled his eyes. "Look, I want to acquaint you with some psychological terminology. Do you know what 'paranoid' means?"

"Don't screw with me. What do *you* think is going on, then?"

"I think that being by yourself and weird hours are getting to you. You need to get another job."

That problem was solved for me. When I went into work that evening, Bob stopped me at the sign-in desk and handed me an envelope. It contained a check and a termination notice. I had somehow been caught copying confidential information off the network. There was no one to blame but myself. I violated their trust in me. The pink slip (no, it wasn't really pink) said that legal action may follow my termination, the case was under study by their attorneys.

Bob was professional, but not unfriendly, as he escorted me to the parking lot.

My severance pay was generous enough for me to sit home and write and watch TV for about a month before I had to find another job. Day by day, I tried to switch my sleep schedule back to something more normal.

A week to the day after I was fired, Jerry and I were in a pub drinking beer and arguing about the possibility of 19th century steam-powered biplanes when I saw a face appear on the TV over the bar. It was the son of the convenience store guy, the somber brown eyes were unmistakable.

I shouted to the bartender. "Turn up the sound!"

"...although the body had not been sexually assaulted. Risal Nizar was six years old." The face of the brown-skinned man appeared on the screen, looking distraught. Beneath the image a caption read, "Marzuki Nizar, victim's father."

"My son....very good boy, very good! What bad person should do this thing? Why?" The grim faced commentator moved on. "In other local-news..."

I turned to Jerry. "That was the kid I told you about!"

"From the 'Kwik-E-Mart'?"

"'Lil' Peach', actually, but yes."

We had to wait for a recap of the report to get the whole story. The cops didn't know exactly what kind of weapon was used in the killing. The child had died from blood loss out of many small wounds. I spite of that, they didn't

believe he had been tortured, rather death had come quickly. His body had been found in his makeshift fort of milk crates.

"Jerry…"

"I swear to freaking God, if you so much as *mention* rats..."

"What the hell else could it be? The kid must have pissed them off in some way, maybe saw something he wasn't supposed to see."

Somehow, I talked him into going with me that night. I'm sure that buying him beer and then shots of Laphroaig for a few hours had something to do with it.

he parking lot was still
and quiet in the muggy night. There were
still police tapes up around the back of
the convenience store. The store itself
was closed. There were no cars in the lot
except for Bob's, so I assumed that they
hadn't found a replacement for me yet.

We parked at the mall rather than in front of Crandall
so that Bob wouldn't notice. He would recognize my car.
I don't know if he would call the cops on me or not, but I
didn't want to find out.

We sat in the car with cups of Burger King coffee for a
few minutes.

"So… what exactly are we looking for?" Jerry politely
inquired.

"Anything weird."

"Weirder than the guy sitting next to me, you mean?"

"Shaddup."

"Nothing weird is going to happen." As if to instantly
make him a liar, there was a tapping on the driver side
window. It was a cop with a flashlight, now shining
directly into my eyes.

"How are you gentlemen tonight?"
he inquired.

"Just fine, officer," I said.

"Are you aware that all of the stores are closed at this hour?"

"We thought we could get some sandwiches at the Lil' Peach," I lied.

"It's closed tonight."

"So we discovered. We were just thinking where to go next."

"There is a Store 24 a mile up the road." The cop pointed with his flashlight. Just then I saw Bob walking toward the car.

"I just came down to see what was going on," he said to the patrolman. And then he recognized me. "Hey Jake!"

"You know this guy?" The cop eyed me.

"Yeah. He just got let go from Crandall last week."

"Crap," I thought.

"Could you gentlemen get out of the car please?," asked the cop politely.

Jerry looked at me with utter disgust. "I'm going to kick your ass."

There was an ID check, and a patdown for Jerry and I. The cop quizzed Bob on everything he knew about me. His responses made me sound like a pretty unsavory character. For some stupid reason "quiet" and "keeps mostly to himself" are red flags to the police.

The officer asked me, "Why did you *really* come out here tonight? It won't help you to lie."

To this day Jerry swears my response made him want to kill me right then and there. I guess I was lucky that he only punched me in the back of the head. "The rats are up to something officer."

After the cop separated and cuffed us both, he came back and asked me to repeat myself. His partner had now stepped out of the cruiser to join us.

"The rats are up to something."

"Is that the best you can do? All I know is that you are some kind of weirdo who just got fired from over there, and now you are back here with a ridiculous explanation at the scene of a sick murder. You understand what this looks like, don't you?"

Up until that second, I didn't, but the implication of what he was getting at suddenly dawned on me. "Are you crazy?!? I didn't kill that kid!"

"Did I say you killed anyone?"

"I saw about it on the news! That's what you think!"

"So now you read minds, and you think the rats are up to something." He looked at his partner significantly, who looked back and twirled an index finger near his temple.

I rolled my eyes when I saw the gesture. "That is *so* unprofessional, officer!"

Jerry said, "Shut up, Jake."

For once in my life, I took good advice and zipped it.

The officer was just holding my head as I was getting into the cruiser when a sound came from the Crandall lot. A fizzing, snapping sound.

There was light coming from in back of the big dumpster. Suddenly, with an explosion and a crash of steel on blacktop, the big steel container overturned spilling trash everywhere. A discarded computer monitor bounced across the lot and landed on the hood of Bob's car, denting it.

"What the fu…" Bob forgot the rest of his sentence. There was a loud hissing noise like escaping gas under pressure and then we saw it. For what it was, it wasn't large, but it was plenty large enough. Floating free of the dumpster, it rose like a great diaphanous cigar the size of a city bus.

It was a rigid frame airship made from things like old umbrella ribs, bicycle spokes, cellophane, egg cartons and a number of small electric motors. It was lit inside and through the translucent envelope, numerous rats could be seen running to and fro.

The cop let go of me and I bumped my head hard on the doorframe. "Son of a bitch!" I yelled.

Jerry was repeating, "You were right, you were right, you were right…" over and over again.

Several of the rats gathered on the side of the dirigible that was closest to us, looking at us. They were now clean and snowy white. It was impossible to read their

expressions, but I had an idea what they were thinking.

"This isn't good," I said.

The airship advanced toward us and dropped down to about twenty feet in altitude. A rat suddenly swung down from the envelope on a salvaged length of lamp cord, right past the face of one of the cops.

There was a bright
reflection from a blade
as the rodent zipped
by the policeman's
face. Blood ran down
his cheek into which a
small letter Z had been
carved.

"Oh my God!" I
said. They had access to
everything that had ever
been on the Crandall
network. Apparently
Zorro had made an
impression.

The cop pulled his
pistol and took a shot at the miniature Zeppelin.

"No!," I yelled. "Don't antagonize them!"

"Why the hell not?!?," exclaimed Jerry, "They killed that kid!"

"Because they'll kill us too, but they can't get far if we just
let them alone."

The other cop, the one who wasn't clutching his face
in pain, asked, "Why not? Why can't they get far?"

I was about to answer when twenty more of
them swung toward us and we had to dive
behind the cop car or be slashed to
bits. I smashed my mouth on
the pavement because the
cuffs held my hands
behind me.

"Son of a bitch!,"
I burbled through my
mouth full of blood.

We heard the tiny
blades scratch the finish
of my car and the cruiser
as they zoomed past. The
rat Zeppelin was directly
overhead. I looked up to see that
there were at least fifty of them,
each and every one too smart for
its own good. It was clear that the
gas envelope was separate from the
section that contained the "crew." I
wondered where they got the helium. Did
it *use* helium?

A smoking Diet Dr. Pepper can dropped
from the sky and rolled under the cruiser.

"Run!" I hollered.

As we all beat it for the trees there was a deep-throated **THUMP!!** The cop car jumped about two feet in the air and hit the pavement hard.

Two heartbeats later, its gas tank exploded.

We felt the heat from forty yards away. The paint on the rear side of my car was totally bubbled.

The cop called to Bob, "Get back to your desk! Call for help!"
The security guard started to hot-foot it back to the building when
another can was ejected from the rogue aircraft. It landed twenty
feet behind him and exploded. Bob lay unconscious, but
apparently in one piece, on the
pavement.

Jerry and I were still in cuffs and I had fallen on my face when the
police car blew up. I hadn't actually broken my nose, but I was bleeding

pretty badly. The
stand of trees was still
fifty yards away.
"Damn it! Can
you PLEASE get
these fucking cuffs off
me?" One of the cops
unlocked Jerry and me
and we both rubbed
our wrists. I touched
my nose gingerly. It
hurt like hell. My lips
were swollen like two
plums, my lower face,
sticky.

The glowing airship swept past us and another smoking can fell into the trees followed by another **THUMP!** Birds (among them, the owl)

exploded out of the branches

and the cat came running out and vanished into the distance like demons from Hell were after it. I suppose, from his perspective, they were. One of the cops stood up and emptied his pistol in the direction of the fleeing airship. It had no obvious effect.

I hollered at the cop. "Let it go! All we have to do is follow it."

The police radio was destroyed, but the cops were able to call for back-up on my cell phone.

When some other cruisers and an ambulance arrived on the scene, Jerry and I piled into the back seat of one of the cop cars that took up the chase. One of the cops started to object, but changed his mind and ignored us for the moment. We shot down the road attempting to keep the airship in sight, but ended up losing it. By that time a helicopter had been dispatched.

They decided that their goal was to get the device in tow and then get animal control involved. It was difficult to approach the craft. One attempt resulted in an exploding Pepsi can being launched in their direction. It exploded close enough to the chopper to give it a good nudge.

Around that time, the pilot reported that the flight of the bizarre aircraft was becoming increasingly erratic. Within a few minutes the dirigible seemed to be no longer under intelligent guidance. It drifted listlessly with only one of the small motors still running, lending it a slow, off-center spin. An hour later, it hung nose down about thirty feet above a residential street in Framingham at the mercy of the rare gentle breezes. Inside the rats were milling around, sleeping or brawling with one another.

I had figured correctly. The rats were no longer a threat.

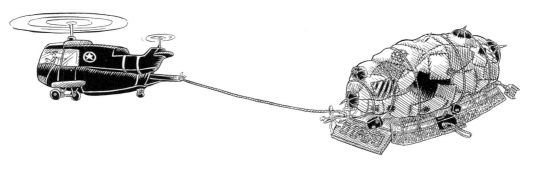

The police helicopter slowly and carefully towed the delicate, makeshift aircraft to a State police station where all of the rats could be captured and contained.

Crandall Labs had a *herd* of lawyers there an hour before dawn. They were claiming that the rats and the "artifact" were property of Crandall Laboratories, Incorporated and should be released to them immediately. They were laughed out of the station. The airship and the rats were evidence in several assaults and a possible homicide. At very least, the matter had to be reviewed by animal control before the disposition of the rats could be decided.

On the surface there did not appear to be anything out of the ordinary about the rats, save for the fact that many of them had tiny swords strapped to them and one of them was wearing corrective lenses on its eyes. One was sacrificed and dissected. An electronic device was discovered in its abdomen with a cable running into its brainstem. X-rays revealed that the others carried similar devices. Crandall's lawyers would not reveal what the devices were, claiming that they represented a proprietary trade secret. The claim wouldn't stand up in court, but it would buy time for the Crandall execs to circle their wagons.

I discovered that Crandall was also planning to sue me for making public information from their network. That was because of the interview I gave a reporter from channel seven, but that happened the next day. That was a "damned if you do, damned if you don't" situation. I ultimately figured that I would rather be sued by Crandall than be charged with obstruction of justice.

I was given a ride to the hospital to get my poor abused face looked at. All I needed was a few stitches in my lower lip, some cotton up my nose and advice from the doctor not to lead with my chin. Very funny.

Jerry put a cup of coffee in front of me.

"I am so sorry for doubting you, dude."

"Ah, don't worry about it. I wouldn't have believed me either."

"So what happened to them? They had it made, they could have escaped."

"Nope, they never had a chance."

"Why? All they had to do was find a hiding place."

"I know what you're thinking, but you saw those critters, those were *not* super rats."

"I admit that they didn't seem to be."

"Those rats were *wired*. They were linked to the Crandall computer network by those devices implanted in them. That's how they were able to seem brainy, but all their information was from the computers. They were using that information to fulfill some sort of rat agenda, or even some weird notion from the computer itself. They seemed to have read my book."

"But why did they stop?"

"Range," I said. "The range of the transmitters in the network appliances was really short, less than a couple of miles. They could only carry a small battery. It couldn't give the signal much **oomph**."

"They got stupid when they got far enough away!"

"Yeah. I wonder how it happened. Did they all lose the connection around the same time, or did they lose it one by one? I wonder if any of them were able to grasp how they had screwed up."

The parking lot of Crandall labs was still overrun with police, hazmat workers (because the rats had been declared a biohazard) and reporters, *lots* of reporters.

A couple of tow trucks with winches were working to right the overturned dumpster and another was jacking up the civilian and police vehicles that had been damaged to be taken away.

In a drainpipe beneath the dumpster hid a single, brooding white rat. Alone with its thoughts, it planned for the future. Nearby processors fed him the language and the concepts to wrap around his vague rodent train of thought.

"The forces of evil have me cornered. They are smugly confident that I have been defeated, but they are wrong. Evil is always wrong, for once again shall rise son of Zorro!"

The End

This story is dedicated to my old pal, Rob Chalfen, who has listened to me say some pretty weird stuff over morning coffee, who really does dream about 78's from another dimension and who introduced me to my first dish of parlor beans.

23. Therefore the Lord God sent him forth from the Garden of Eden to till the ground from whence he was taken.

24. And the dog, Aruf, appealed to the Lord. "Oh Lord, may I too journey from the garden with Adam, for I am his true companion and he shelters me and I am his friend. Beyond the garden I shall guard him and keep him."

25. And the Lord replied, "You have not sinned against me and still you may have a place in paradise. Why should you wish to suffer pain and death and the travails of the accursed?"

26. And Aruf replied, "The man and all his generation shall need of my loyalty and my trueness to remind them of your loyalty and your truth."

27. And the Lord God said unto Aruf, "So it shall be that you and your generations shall walk by the side of man and his generations, and I shall let you and your generations continue to have sensible speech when all other four footed beasts shall not, so that a righteous voice shall always be heard in the world.

28. So he drove out the man and the dog walked by his side. And he placed at the east of the garden of Eden Cherubims and a flaming sword which turned every way to keep the way of the tree of life.
        ~ Genesis, Chapter 3

Children of Aruf

BY Seth Kallen Deitch

Garf slept by the stove. He neither kicked nor whined nor did any of the things that so many dogs tended to when unconscious. His was the sleep of the innocent. Had Jack not known him so well, he would have been tempted to take his pulse.

The dog stirred, stretched and raised his head. "Gotta pee, Jack," he mumbled. The dog got up stretching and yawning.

Jack was at the table cleaning his brushes. "So who's stopping you?"

"C'mon, Jack, I want you to come out with me. It's a beautiful day."

"Garf, who leads the pack?"

Garf bowed his head slightly. "You do, Jack."

"So just go pee then."

Garf walked toward the door, tail hanging down. He turned back. "Jack?"

Jack looked up from his work again. "Yes?"

"C'mon out. Please?"

Jack knew Garf wouldn't let up until he went with him. He tossed his brushes in the can of turpentine and started putting his shoes on.

When they got outside it was hot and humid and it had rained that morning. Even to Jack's human nose, the air was redolent with redolence. Garf whirled around. "Wow! So much…*everything!*" Jack envied Garf's smell picture of the world. He had, on occasion, tried to make him jealous of his own full-color vision. The canine could not have cared less. Besides, his attention span was too short for him to really get into deep descriptions of art or sunsets before he would catch a whiff of a squirrel or a bitch and no longer be listening. People who don't know dogs well, and there are some, think that they can talk to dogs like they do to people, which is laughable. Dogs have never been deep thinkers. Throughout history there have never been dog philosophers, or dog novelists or dog scientists, but there *have* been many dog poets and dog saints. Their strength was love and loyalty and a natural honesty. It is commonly said that they never lie and they never cheat and are deeply perplexed if they are lied to or cheated on. It's not really true, but dogs are notably *bad* at lying and cheating and only tend to get away with it with other dogs. In general, dogs are credited with great faithfulness and nobility and a capacity for unconditional love.

Jack's Garf was the most noble of them all. Jack had been painting him lately, four canvases so far. He wanted to capture that spark of his soul that made him so special.

Garf was whelped by his sister's companion, Grna. It was she who named him Garf. In modern times, in the western nations, dogs use names given by the bitch that birthed them, but that has not always been so. In times past, humans would give them romantic, symbolic or even cute names, but the German dog poet Ur-narf (*né Flaumig*) urged dogs to use their, what was then known as "mother names" or "bitch names," as their primary identifier.

The puppy Garf loved Jack almost as soon as his eyes had opened and learned to call his name when he was only ten weeks old. Grna brought him to Jack when he was weaned and, by custom, he knew that he had to take young Garf even though he was on his way to college in a month. That was seven years ago and Garf was now in prime middle age. He had a pretty large vocabulary, twice that of the average dog, but tended to misuse words a lot. Jack would frequently hear "pedicure" when Garf meant "pedestrian" or "light-bulb" for "lighter."

He was handsome. Grna had been a golden retriever, but she never said who had gotten the pups on her. She probably wasn't sure herself. Whoever he had been, he was also a large dog, probably some sort of mastiff. Garf had a high fore-head and deep, intelligent, golden eyes. He was burly and shaggy with dark brown fur save for one white rear leg and a white streak across one eye. To Jack, he was one of the finest of the sons of Aruf.

After his initial pirouette outside the door, Garf sprinted off, covering a hundred yards in the blink of an eye.

"What is it, Garf?" Called Jack.

The dog's voice came back faintly, "Dunno. Woochuck, maybe." Jack noticed that he seemed to have totally forgotten about his bladder.

There came a surprised bark and then a howl! Jack started running as fast as he could to where he had last seen the dog. "Garf! Are you alright?" He called. He heard a whine from behind a shrub. Looking around he saw Garf with a miserable expression and a defeated posture. He had several porcupine quills in his nose and lips.

"I was stupid, Jack." He said.

"Damn it, Garf. You scared me, I thought you were really hurt!"

"It *does* hurt, Jack. Make it stop."

"Yeah, yeah…come along, big fella."

They went back to the house and Jack carefully pulled out the spines and dabbed the punctures with Oragel. Garf hated the smell, but tolerated it because it helped the pain. Jack also gave him a slice of salami that seemed to make Garf forget the whole episode. They watched a baseball game together although Garf snoozed through much of it. He only really paid attention when Pittsburgh was playing because of Kraulo, his favorite fetcher, being in the outfield. Jack was more into the human players because he was interested in batting averages.

As Garf slept, Jack, for some reason, found himself thinking of his first companion, Olo, who had been killed when he was thirteen. Olo had been completely different from Garf, calm and deliberate where Garf was spirited and playful. In retrospect, he reminded Jack of Servius, Hamlet's sage companion in the famous Shakespeare play. The role had always been played by a human on stage because he had too many lines for a dog to remember, but in the film with Lawrence Olivier, Craghoph, the first great dog actor of talking pictures, played the role because he only had to remember a few lines at a time. Olo didn't have the noble profile of Craghoph, but he did have Servius' commonsense wisdom. Olo died because he was old and going deaf and didn't hear a car coming. Young Jack was heartbroken and swore not to keep another dog, but Garf was brought to him and loved him unconditionally from the first moment.

Jack looked over at Garf. He kicked in his sleep and muttered. "Got you, porky... rrrrrrr." He snorted and kicked again, "not so tough without quills, are ya?" Jack laughed, but no so loudly he would wake his friend from so nice a dream.

Jack went into the city once a month to check in with a gallery that showed his work. Venues like this have sold a painting of two for him in the past, but not so many that he could give up his job.

The train to Boston was not as crowded as Jack had seen it on some days, but plenty crowded enough for his taste. Garf spent most of his time in the front of the car with a few other dogs only occasionally making the rounds of the seats politely asking passengers if they had any treats they wanted to share. Most dogs cannot be dissuaded from mooching and most of their companions give up trying pretty early in the game. A dog's master would merely discipline him if he got too pushy, that is if the victims of his attentions didn't do so first. Jack just hoped that Garf would take no for an answer and not get himself cuffed on the head too many times. Begging was really only considered cute in puppies.

Garf stopped by the seat of a young woman who was eating a salami sandwich. He *loved* salami. He gave her the big eyes and then caught a slight whiff of something else. He put on his most innocent voice. "Excuse me miss, why did you leave your dog at home?" He was hoping that she, in fact, hadn't and that the bitch was somewhere else on the train.

The woman looked at him and smiled. She was well aware that dogs knew things that were invisible to humans. "I think you know why."

Garf wasn't really too slick. He had tipped his hand that he had smelled bitch in heat on the woman. He grinned sheepishly.

"I know it's second best, but would you like some salami?"

"Nice lady!" said Garf wagging his tail with enthusiasm.

Garf came by Jack's seat and put his paws on the arm. Leaning into his face he said "Hi Jack!"

"Sweet Jesus, Garf! What the hell have you been eating?"

"Garlic and pepper dry salami!"

"Well, stop breathing it on me, if you don't mind!"

Feldma's gallery-café was on the corner of Essex and Newbury Street, just a short subway ride from North Station.

Ron Rosenberg called himself "Feldma" for business purposes. The old painted sign over the door had never been removed since the place had been "Feldman's Spa and Sandwich" back in the '60s. The distressed sign now simply said "Feldma," the N having been erased by decades of weather, with the word "Gallery" added by a graffiti artist directly on top of the words "spa and sandwich." The name was established and in his mind it was catchier than Rosenberg.

When they entered Feldma waved and said, "You have *two* sales!"

Jack grinned in response as did Garf, even though he didn't "get" Jack's work.

Feldma continued. "Word is spreading, my friend. *Everyone* is going to want an original Jackson Hayes!"

"*Everyone*? Let's not get carried away."

Feldma put his fists on his hips like a scolding mother. "Everyone who's any-one!" The gallery owner leaned down nose to nose with Garf. "And how is Garfy-warfy today?" He cooed. "*How* is Garfy-warfy?!?"

Garf growled and snapped his jaws an inch from Feldma's nose. Feldma pulled his face back in alarm and snarled, "Savage!"

"C'mon, Feldma, you know he hates baby talk." Feldma wasn't good with dogs.

"Thinks I'm a dumb puppy," muttered Garf.

"S'ok, buddy. He didn't mean anything by it."

Feldma composed himself. Jack found his attitude reminiscent of Margaret Dumont. "Anyway," he continued, "I want to show at least five more pieces immediately."

Jack was delighted. If he continued like this he might be able to go part-time at the bookstore. With check in pocket, he and Garf left the gallery.

Garf wanted to go to the Dog's Haven at Trinity Church. Dogs enjoyed worship in large groups so whenever he got a chance, Garf went to a big-city church.

The Dog's Haven was a separate chapel within the great church. It was impressive looking although the colors were muted in recognition of canine monochrome vision. On the wall above the altar hung a crucifix with suffering Christ and mourning dog at the base of the cross. There is much folklore about Saint Natra (called Naythus in the Roman church, his doggish name is lost to history), the canine companion of Jesus, although he is only referred to a few times in the gospels and then only briefly. There is in fact a whole Gospel of Natra arising from the Gnostic tradition that tells of his ministry after the crucifixion of Jesus and his own eventual martyrdom by stoning. The stoning of Natra has long been a popular theme for painters, the most famous version being that of Artemisia Gentileschi. In her version, the stoning is shown taking place at sunrise with deep chiaroscuro shadows. Half in shadow stands Natra, a rope around his neck tying him to an iron ring set in a stone wall. The first stone has struck him and some blood shows on his ribs. The canine saint looks up in pain and resignation and with forgiveness for his executioners. The man who has thrown the first stone points to show the injury he has done. A bored-looking Roman soldier stands to one side. It was one of Jack's favorite paintings.

Humans tended to find the chapel had an unpleasant odor because worshipers always marked with a few drops of urine upon entering. On major holidays, many humans would find it almost impossible to enter, but that was not the case today. There were only about twenty dogs in the large room, all of them flat on their bellies before the altar as the dog priest delivered his sermon. Garf went up and prostrated himself on the floor while Jack seated himself in a pew near the back. Jack was raised Episcopalian, but didn't attend church often and considered himself agnostic. Garf, like most dogs whatever their faith, was intensely devout.

The priest was speaking of duty. "We are called to run with God's pack, one and all and to submit to his ways and will. To stray from the pack of God is to forget our duty." At this, the congregation laid back their ears and emitted soft howls. "Even the mightiest leader of the largest pack will joyfully show his belly to the almighty!" The entire congregation rolled over exposing their undersides and barked lustily.

Jack understood that this was very moving for dogs. To him it seemed silly, not that he would ever consider saying so in Garf's presence.

After Garf had his fill of sacred groveling, he and Jack took a walk through the Public Garden before taking the train back north. Garf reveled in the festival of strange scents that Jack was blind to and kept running off to and fro to discover their origins. Jack indulged him and just enjoyed the Garden.

"Jack!" His name was called and he looked to see Bill Davis coming his way led by Garf. "Look who I found, Jack!" exclaimed the dog.

"Damn, Jack! It's been an age!" Bill gave Jack an almost painful bear hug.

"Bill, what the hell have you been doing?"

"Web design for WGBH."

"So, no work today?"

"Nah, I have Mondays off. I'm free as an Irish dog today. Do you want to grab lunch?"

"I can't today, we have to get back, but I'll be down again next weekend and we'll do something then if you have the time." They made plans to do just that and Jack and Garf got on the Subway for North Station.

As they waited for the train, Garf asked, "Why do people say that, Jack?"

"Say what?"

"Free as an Irish dog."

"Oh. Well, you know that a dog must have a master or a mistress?"

"Yeah, sure."

"Across the ocean is the country of Ireland, You've heard of it?"

"Where they make the delicious black beer!" Jack had given Garf a little saucer of Guinness on certain special occasions.

"That's right. Well, in Ireland about a hundred and fifty years ago they made a law that said a dog didn't have to have a master and had to be paid for any work he did and could own property. It's the only place in the world where a masterless dog can live among people. People say 'free as an Irish dog' to mean that no one has a claim on their time."

"I don't understand. I'm free, aren't I?"

"I'm responsible for you as your companion and technically, I own you, but it is more like I'm responsible for your welfare the way a parent is responsible for a child. As a bitch must guard the welfare of her pups so a master must guard the welfare of his dog. That is how it has always been."

"So what do the Irish dogs do?"

"Most of them live as we do although many more dogs work for a living in Ireland, mostly herding sheep, and those that do, get paid for it. They end up giving all their money back to humans because dogs don't have hands so it makes more sense for them to pay humans to make things for them than to make them themselves. Dogs can hunt, but there is little free game in Ireland so they must mostly buy food. Dogs can't read or write so they don't want things like newspapers and books. Dog freedom in human society is mostly pointless."

"It is?"

"What would you do if you were 'free as an Irish dog'?"

"I don't know. I'm in your pack. I would still be in your pack if I was free."

"And I would still be in yours."

Jack was actually unsure of the strength of his argument, but Garf, as far as he could follow it, accepted the reasoning. Jack noted to himself that this had been the first time he had discussed politics with Garf or any dog.

It was two month's later that Bill came up to visit Jack. He was happy to get out of the city for a weekend and the famous autumn foliage of the region was at its peak.

Bill had known Garf as a puppy and adolescent dog when he was in college with Jack and Garf remembered him fondly. On that Saturday, Garf insisted on leading Bill around the neighborhood. It worked out because Bill could take in some of the fall colors and Garf could nose around to his heart's content. Jack's place was an old farm house and the extensive yard had been a farm once upon a time. The land had not been worked since before the Second World War and, except for a tended area around the house itself and the driveway, had been completely overgrown with tall grass for many decades. Of course Garf loved to romp through the wild parts of the farm and he led Bill into some of his favorite places. He was just babbling on about how this tree had a really big family of squirrels or there was a rabbit warren ahead or that he knew where there was a dead raccoon, etc. Bill just said "uh-huh" a lot while he simply enjoyed the walk and Garf's enthusiasm even if he wasn't fascinated with his narrative. Garf looked over at him at one point just in time to see him suddenly drop into the Earth. He barked in alarm and dashed over to the spot where Bill had vanished. There was a hole in the ground and pieces of broken wood. An old rotted board over an unused well had given way under Bill's weight. Garf looked into the hole, but all he could see was darkness. "Bill!," he called. He repeated Bill's name several more times before he finally heard a groan of pain from far below.

"Garf...what happened?"

"You fell down a hole! Are you o.k.?"

Garf heard Bill moving and then a cry of pain. He finally spoke in a thin, weak voice. "I think my leg is broken pretty bad."

"Don't move, Bill. I'll go get Jack!"

The dog bolted back for the house as fast as he could leaping over rocks and mounds of tall grass. He ran full speed into the house and found Jack at his easel. He tried to speak but the words tripped over one another in an incoherent jumble and he started barking in frustration.

"Good Lord, Garf! What is it? Calm down and tell me!"

Garf subsided a bit and just sat and panted for a few seconds. Finally he was able to speak. "Bill fell down a wall!"

"Fell down a wall? Do you mean *off* a wall?"

"A wall, a wall! A hole in the ground for water!"

"A *well*! Holy shit! Is he alright?"

"He's trapped and he's got a broken leg."

"Take me to him!"

The fire department got Bill out, but it took some time. His leg was broken in several places and he was going to walk with a cane for the rest of his life even after it healed, but he was alive. Jack was horrified. He had the well filled in. He had sold enough paintings to afford to have the entire property cleared by a landscaping company. It was now less fun for Garf, but a lot safer. For a long time Jack felt guilt over what had happened.

Winter came and winter went. Jack kept in close touch with Bill and, almost as a consequence of the mishap, their friendship strengthened. As Spring turned to Summer, another change came to Jack and Garf's lives when Jack married a local bartender, Sharon, who had a canine companion of her own, Krowl. Suddenly, the old farm seemed a lot more like a home. The two dogs became fast friends and they both looked to Jack as top dog in the pack, even though Sharon seemed to be in charge of Jack.

That Thanksgiving, they had Bill and his girlfriend as guests and after dinner Jack and Bill sat down with cocktails just to let the turkey stupor pass.

"Ya' know, Bill, I still think about it every day."

"Think about what?"

"The accident. What might have happened."

"Garf was with me. I was always going to be alright."

"Sometimes I wonder. I mean what if dogs were just like all the other animals?"

Bill looked at him strangely. "They are like other animals."

"No they're not. They talk. We're used to it. We never really think about it, but only humans and dogs talk. If Garf couldn't talk, you would have died that day."

"Oh, I'm not so sure. There was a kid's TV show, I think it was based on a book, about a deaf-mute collie that always was able to tell humans when her master, a little boy named Timmy, was in trouble. Sometimes he would be treed by a mountain lion. Once he was even trapped down a well, but Lassie always got help!"

"Lassie? Odd name for a dog."

"She was a deaf-mute adopted after her previous master died in an accident. She was never able to tell her real mother name, so her new master called her Lassie. In the series she was played by a dog with normal hearing."

"It seems pretty contrived. Still, I'm glad that Garf can talk, even if he doesn't have much to say sometimes, I'm still glad for his voice."

52 .Loyal Before the Lord we are
and with his pack we run always.
For we are the faithful, we are the loyal
and we stand beside his table for
he will feed and nurture us and
he will lead us into paradise.
53. So let us show not only our
belly to the Lord, but also a joyful tail.

- The Gnostic gospel of Natra, chapter 5

was just a little kid the first time I heard that song. Like a lot of old songs from before my time, I first heard it and a lot of old chestnuts just as arcane from the old cartoons they used to show on TV.

I've always felt I missed out on a lot of cool old things by being born too late, but I was right there when TV first got rolling. And back then the cartoons we saw on TV were either from the silent days or from the very dawn of talking pictures.

The ones with sound were loaded with old time songs; everything from "Moonlight Bay" and "I'm Forever Blowing Bubbles" to "Yes We Have No Bananas."

That ditty about the cop on the beat and the man in the moon came from an old Van Beuren cartoon made in New York City back in 1932.

Anyway, this story isn't about old cartoons. It does take place in New York City but a lot later than 1932; 1968 to be exact, at which time I was a young man living on New York's Lower East side.

I was just getting my so-called career as a comic strip artist off the ground working for an underground newspaper called The East Village Other. The hippy era was in full cry,

HEY! WHAT'S WITH ALL THE BLANK PAGES UP THERE!

HEY MAN, KEEP YOUR SHIRT ON.

Wednesday paste up night at The East Village Other circa 1968.

Art director, Don Lewis.

Me, under the gun as usual.

My friend and colleague, SPAIN.

Our tough guy boss, the great Joel Fabricant.

and I was pretty much right in the middle of it.

Me in '68 — Born, 1944

Went to art school for a few years but didn't really fit in. Knocked around in the Norwegian merchant marine for a little while and went through a series of straight jobs ending up as an attendant at a nut house where a revelation on the graveyard shift got me back on the art track around 1965.

I'd quit my last straight job in Westchester and migrated to the Lower East side about a year before. And, all things considered, I wasn't doing too bad.

I was pulling down forty a week, real money at The East Village Other. Not so bad when you consider that flats down there were going on average for about fifty a month.

Like most of 'em, mine was a cockroach-infested dump that required my carrying a loaded gun just to keep the junkies off my back, coming and going from it. But I knew plenty of other people down there who weren't doing as good as me.

And I knew a few who were doing better, like

(Forget it. He's packing.)

my buddy Mark. He'd preceded me in the migration from Westchester by about six months and lucked into a pretty good situation playing guitar in a group called "Groovination." They played these big "happening" style gigs at a ballroom in Midtown and were doing decent business. The band hung together commune style, in a loft over on seventh street and First Avenue. I used to go over there not so much to see Mark as to moon over the band's singer, a stunning girl named Cheryl Stein.

As a singer, Cheryl was no Janis Joplin, but she more than got by on her dark good looks. Based on no real evidence, I'd somehow convinced myself that maybe

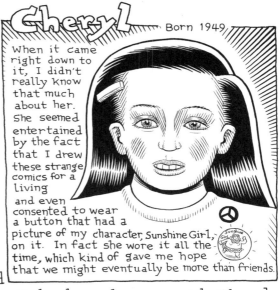

Cheryl — Born 1949

When it came right down to it, I didn't really know that much about her. She seemed entertained by the fact that I drew these strange comics for a living and even consented to wear a button that had a picture of my character, Sunshine Girl, on it. In fact she wore it all the time, which kind of gave me hope that we might eventually be more than friends.

I had a chance with Cheryl.

She liked me well enough to go to a party or the occasional movie with me, but the plain fact is, I was putting a lot of energy into a situation that wasn't really going anywhere.

One thing that was keeping hope alive was that I couldn't see any real competition on the horizon. Still, for that fast and loose era, the situation was kind of pathetic, really.

Looking back, the main thing Cheryl and I seemed to have in common was that neither of us really quite fit into the hippy scene.

We were both more like fellow travelers,

more attracted to the cutting edge status of the hippy movement back then than anything else about it.

So that was pretty much the situation one spring day in '68 when I was heading over to Groovination's Loft. Like most days heading over there, I could already hear the twang of their electric guitars rehearsing a good half block before I got there. Usually I could also hear the wailing of La Lupe, The Queen Of Latin Soul, blasting off a neighboring radio in angry competition. Usually I'd also hear a certain amount of Spanish cursing and grumbling over Groovination's arrogant intrusion into their neighborhood, but not this day.

What I was hearing from the band already sounded subtly but distinctly better; more together. The tune was new too; bluesy and swingy. When I got inside, I saw right away what the difference was.

itting in with the band, playing a guitar borrowed from Wesley, the band's lead guitar player was a fat old guy, about fifty to fifty-five years old I'd say, wearing the gray fatigue uniform of a janitor or handyman of some kind.

By his feet was a half empty half pint of Wilson's "That's All", just about the cheapest blended whiskey you could get back then.

And the old boy wasn't passing up any of the various joints making their way through the room either.

Nope, he wasn't passing up a thing and he wasn't missing a beat on that catchy tune he was banging out either. The tune turned out to be something called "The Crazy Blues," and he sang a chorus of it too. He said he wrote it himself although in later years I found out it wasn't true.* So maybe a lot of what he said also wasn't true.

Anyway, when the tune was over, he took another slug from that half pint of Wilson's, pocketed the rest, had another hit off one of the joints floating through the room, handed Wesley back his guitar and split.

From the guys in the *"Crazy Blues"©1920 PERRY BRADFORD

band I learned his name was Charlie and that he was some kind of a handyman at one of the warehouses on the block.

Apparently he'd drifted over, attracted by the band's rehearsing, and after listening to his tall talk, they let him sit in. That was about a week before and he'd been coming around ever since. Not that the band was exactly overwhelmed by Charlie. It wasn't like they'd found an old black blues man from way down South. This guy was a little harder for them to peg than that.

"Crazy Blues" notwithstanding, left to his own devices, Charlie would revert to a sweeter, croonier singing style, more of a hip tin pan alley kind of thing than Jazz or blues; never mind rock n' roll. Consequently, besides being good for the price of a cheap half pint and a few hits of pot, the guys pretty much regarded Charlie with a good deal of condescension.

However, I was soon to learn that this did not extend to Cheryl.

My mission that day was to see if Cheryl would go out with me later on. Mysteriously, she told me she had something on that night, but if I wanted to call for her around seven, I could come with her.

Where she took me that night was to a warehouse at the other end of the block. After she knocked at a locked door there, it opened and there was Charlie!

I had to admit it wasn't what I was expecting though at that moment I was thinking it sure could have been a lot worse.

I mean, let's face it, the guy was almost old enough to be Cheryl's grandfather, so he couldn't really be regarded as competition.

It turned out that Charlie was regarded more as a night watch-man than a handyman and pretty soon we were sitting in this tiny rat's nest of a room way in back where he apparently lived.

I was feeling surer and surer of myself. Charlie's room even smelled bad. But I got used to it pretty fast. Charlie'd laid in a big old jug of wine and pretty soon we all had a good glow on from it. Meanwhile, Charlie was canoodling around on an old beat up acoustic guitar he had, singing and yarning about his younger life.

Charlie's guitar was so small it might have actually been a kid's toy.

Well, I was pretty sure it was a yarn, but I had to admit it was a good one.

I was entertained even though much to my growing dismay, Cheryl seemed totally enthralled. And through it all he sang bits and pieces of popular songs of a bygone era;

melodic, romantically subdued songs that I vaguely associated with the 1930's. Occasionally there would be something I vaguely recognized like "Where The Blue Of The Night Meets The Gold Of The Day."

I knew that one was old Bing Crosby's theme song. Bing, the singing idol of the 1930's, still reprised that one on occasional TV specials aimed mostly at the * Geritol set.

... Someone waits for me ♫

Then there was "Learn To Croon." Cheryl and I both recognized that one. Alfalfa sings it to Darla in one of those Little Rascals shorts they were still showing in '68.

And then, WOW! There it was!

WAIT, I KNOW. HERE'S A CUTE ONE.

* Geritol. Circa 1960's medicine for old folks.

Out of nowhere, Charlie suddenly launched into nothing less than "The Cop On The Beat, The Man In The Moon And Me", the goofy song from that ancient old cartoon!

Around th' corner there's a party upstairs, here on the corner are we, ♪

I nudged Cheryl, but she was mesmerized and I never did find out if she'd seen that cartoon.

The fact is, he had us both enthralled with wild tales of an era long gone, the early 30's, when crooners were king and Bing Crosby was the king of them all. Charlie seemed to have the inside scoop on it all too. He told us he once split a joint with Bing in a dressing room at the New York Paramount Theatre.

YOUNG BING

YOUNG CHARLIE

AH, CHARLIE MY BOY!

Charlie told us he was filling in that day for Eddie Lang Bing's regular guitarist.

He was full of wild stories; not just about Crosby, but his crooner competition too. Guys I'd never heard of like Russ Columbo, Bing's biggest rival.

Russ Columbo, 1908 1934

Charlie said Columbo didn't swing like Crosby, but he made the girls just as weak in the knees as Bing did, and he launched into a little bit of a Columbo song, "Prisoner Of Love," by way of example.

Charlie told us Columbo would have been as big as Bing but for his untimely demise in 1934. Columbo was in a room having a heated conversation with a man said to be his best friend. The friend struck a match on an antique pistol to light a smoke. A long forgotten charge in the gun went off. A ball ricocheted off a desk and right into Columbo's left eye!

Bing Crosby

COLUMBO'S ADORE BAMBINO
Baby of Family Now Topnotch Crooner

Russ

IN THIS CORNER! Russ Columbo, crooning baritone, who once was in the same orchestra with Crosby and now is a screen and radio star in his own right.

Sept. 2, 1934. Lansing Brown stares in shock as an antique pistol, thought to be unloaded, unexpectedly goes off.

Oddly this puff piece appeared that morning in an L.A. Newspaper.

Is Russ "contemplating the indescribable void"* in this photo taken shortly before his death?

*Joseph Lanza in "Russ Columbo and the Crooner Mystique"
© 2002 Feral House Press

Charlie took a swig and told us confidentially that Russ and his friend had been more than friends and that his death was no accident.

IF YOU KNOW WHAT I MEAN.

And he went on to describe even more obscure figures of that era. A singer named Harlan Lattimore, who might have been as big as Bing and Russ except he was black.

HARLAN LATTIMORE

1908 - 1971

"THE BLACK CROSBY"

He sang with the Don Redman Band and could croon with the best. However, being black and, over time, not too reliable, he is not very well remembered today; great singer, though.

DON REDMAN

OH MY, YES. HE WAS TROUBLE ITSELF. IN A WAY I HATED TO SEE HIM GO BUT, YOU KNOW, THE SHOW MUST GO ON.

Or Chick Bullock, who, oddly, was only photographed in profile and consistently recorded with the best jazz men in town.

And then there was Charlie's own career. Yeah, Charlie made some sides too, he said.

I WASN'T SO HARD TO LOOK AT IN THOSE DAYS, he said with a sly wink at Cheryl. And the smile on her face as she gazed back up at him had me good and worried.

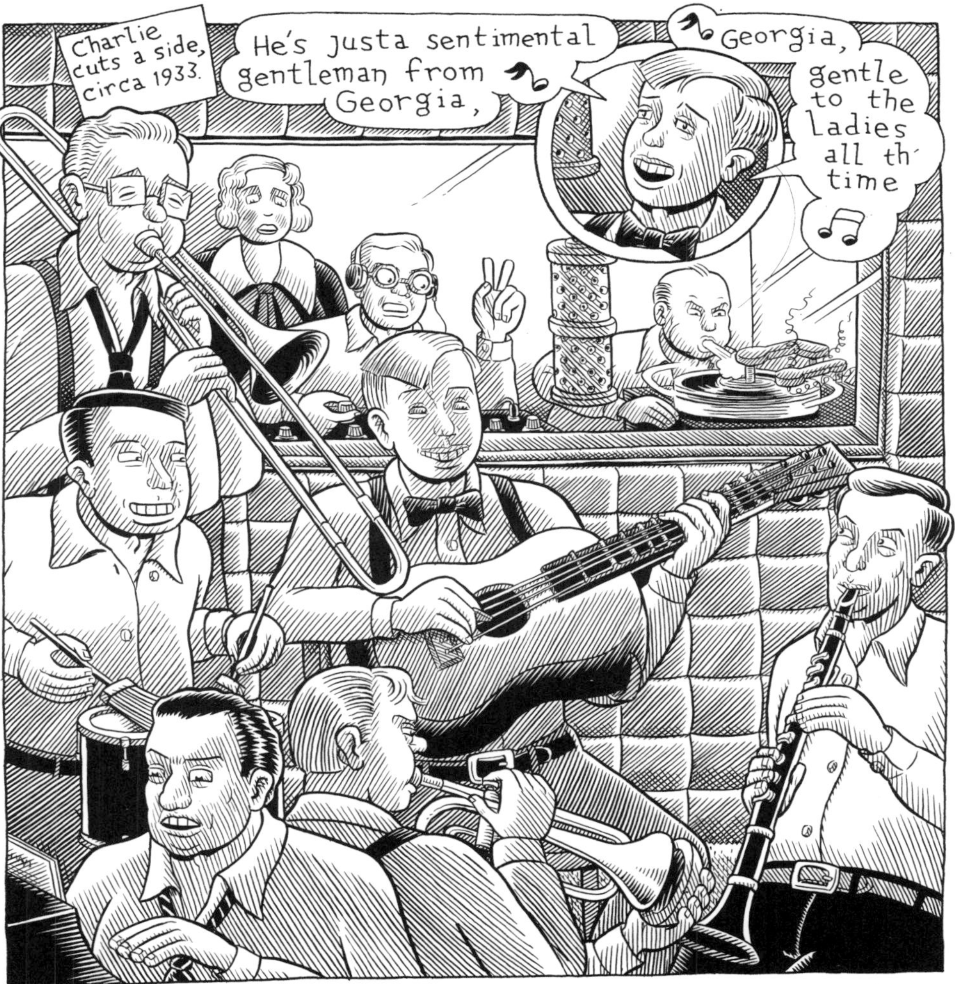
Charlie cuts a side, circa 1933.
He's justa sentimental gentleman from Georgia,
Georgia,
gentle to the ladies all th' time

Clearly there was a growing vibe between them that was starting to crowd me right out of Charlie's small stinky room.

Was it all bullshit? Maybe some of it, but to this day I'm just not sure. But he had our undivided attention as he launched into his own checkered story.

John Dillinger, trying to have some fun, but pretty sure his days are numbered; and he's right.

Pretty Boy Floyd. Things haven't been going so good since he got flushed out of the Cookson Hills.

POTAWATAME LODGE

POTAWATAME

MAY 1934

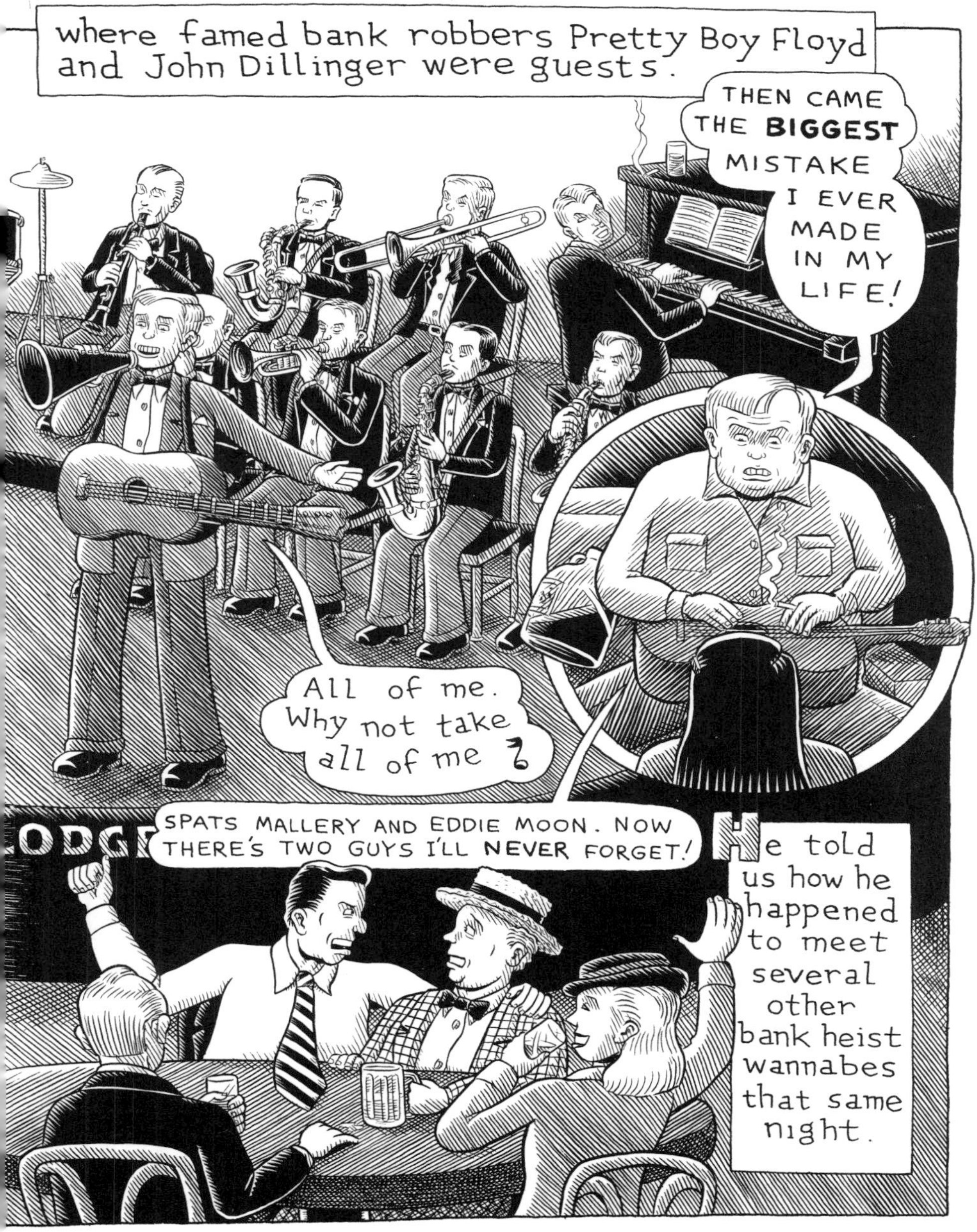
where famed bank robbers Pretty Boy Floyd and John Dillinger were guests.
THEN CAME THE **BIGGEST** MISTAKE I EVER MADE IN MY LIFE!
All of me. Why not take all of me
ODGE
SPATS MALLERY AND EDDIE MOON. NOW THERE'S TWO GUYS I'LL **NEVER** FORGET!
He told us how he happened to meet several other bank heist wannabes that same night.

How they set him up as a street singing distraction in an attempted bank robbery just outside of Kansas City that went terribly wrong.

The would be robbers were killed outrigt and Charlie was nabbed. Worse yet, all the stolen money was gone.

HEY, I'M NO ANGEL BUT I WAS FRAMED JUST AS PRETTY AS YOU PLEASE!

I wasn't sure how much of any of this I believed, except for the jail part. He did have a sort of

vaguely preserved old-prisoner look to him when you thought about him in that way. And he did say he'd been in prison pretty much ever since. Whatever the real truth was, the look in Charlie's eye told me

he wanted Cheryl and it was all I could do to get her out of there! Not that it did me one bit of good. She was still chock full of old Charlie when we finally got out on the street and I knew I was sunk.

What I didn't know and what did surprise me a little was that after that night I never saw Cheryl or Charlie ever again. They were just gone after that. No note. No nothing!

Back at the loft, all her stuff was gone. The band was pretty pissed too.

Her mysterious good looks were definitely a large part of the mix that contributed to their moderate success. And even though I was as crestfallen over her disappearance as they were, irrationally, they seemed to be blaming me.
I guess I did know, somehow, just that much

more about it than they did. I knew she wasn't a crime victim and I knew she wasn't dead. I also knew that wherever she was, she was with Charlie.

The band limped along for another year and then died, more or less of natural causes.

Of course as time went by, I did sometimes wonder what had become of Cheryl and Charlie, especially as I gradually began to discover more about that old music.

Me and rock n' roll never really were a good fit. Oh sure, I like early Elvis, but as rock n' roll gradually evolved into "rock," our national music, that's even played at political conventions, I came to cordially despise it.

Then one day I found an old 78 rpm record of "This Year's Kisses" by "Chick Bullock And His Levee Loungers." And those levee loungers could swing. Over time I discovered that those levee loungers routinely included the likes of the Dorsey brothers and the wailing open trumpet of Bunny Berrigan. Never heard of ♫'s Bunny Berrigan? Well gosh! Do yourself a favor and look into it!

Chick is an acquired taste and I didn't fully appreciate him right away.

This year's crop of kisses

Bunny Berrigan 1908 — 1942

Truly great. He had a solid open horn style reminiscent of young Louis Armstrong. Sadly, he had a booze problem more along the lines of Bix Beiderbecke and he died of it at age 33.

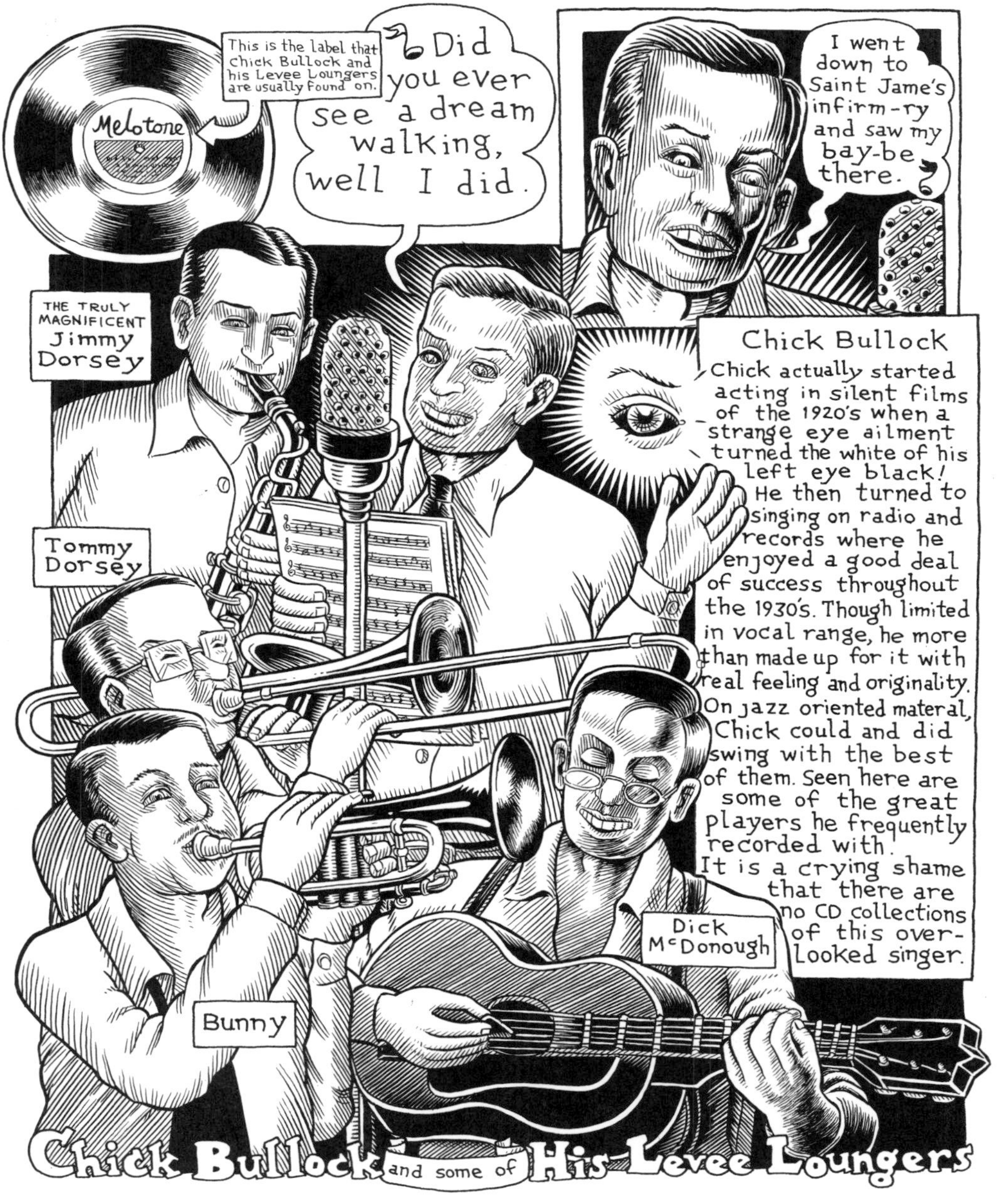
This is the label that Chick Bullock and his Levee Loungers are usually found on.
Melotone
Did you ever see a dream walking, well I did.
I went down to Saint Jame's infirm-ry and saw my bay-be there.
THE TRULY MAGNIFICENT Jimmy Dorsey
Chick Bullock
Chick actually started acting in silent films of the 1920's when a strange eye ailment turned the white of his left eye black! He then turned to singing on radio and records where he enjoyed a good deal of success throughout the 1930's. Though limited in vocal range, he more than made up for it with real feeling and originality. On jazz oriented materal, Chick could and did swing with the best of them. Seen here are some of the great players he frequently recorded with. It is a crying shame that there are no CD collections of this over-looked singer.
Tommy Dorsey
Dick McDonough
Bunny
Chick Bullock and some of His Levee Loungers

And then there's Bing Crosby. Oh sure, he may be only dimly recalled today, if at all, as the old guy who introduced "I'm Dreaming Of A White Christmas." But that was long after his roaring prime; long after the days when he smoked weed with Louis Armstrong and sang with Bix. Don't Know Bix either? Well, check it out!

Bix Beiderbecke
1903 ~ 1931
Cornet player and composer. After Armstrong, Bix was probably the most innovative hot horn player of the 1920's. Unfortunately, his addiction to alcohol eventually undermined his abilities and finally killed him at the young age of 28.

June 10, 1928, New York City. Bing kicks off "Taint So," a tune by Willard Robeson, with Paul Whiteman and his Orchestra for Columbia Record 146316. Take nine!

Bix Beiderbecke, all set to blow some fine cornet.

And Eddie Lang was always playing that stunning guitar with Bing in those days too; until he died. He was only thirty but he must have been camping out in recording studios if the wealth and sheer variety of the sides he left behind are anything to go by.

Eddie Lang had a way of making good singers sound great. Bing knew that. And as truly great as he was, he never did sound

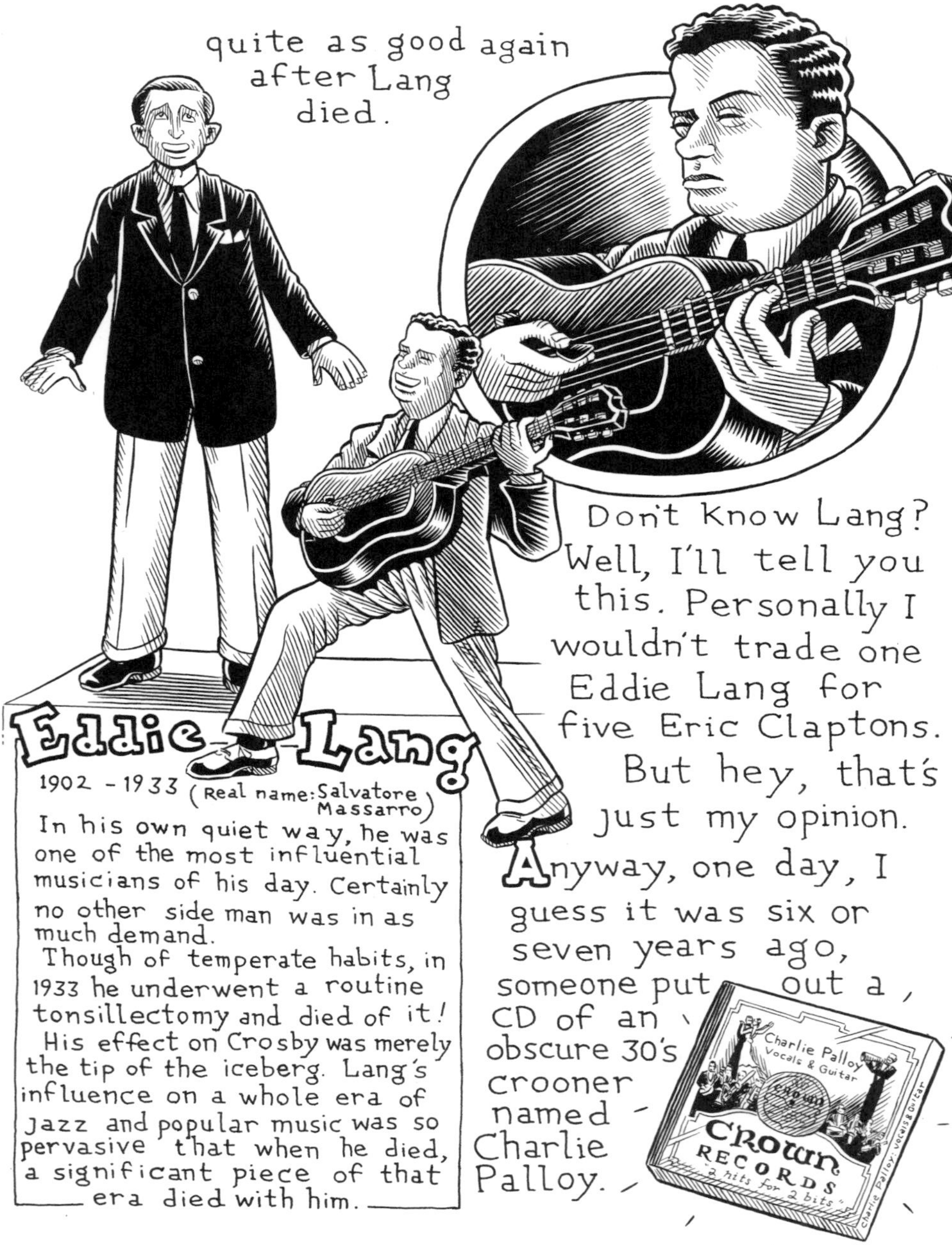
quite as good again after Lang died.
Don't Know Lang? Well, I'll tell you this. Personally I wouldn't trade one Eddie Lang for five Eric Claptons. But hey, that's just my opinion.
Eddie Lang
1902 - 1933 (Real name: Salvatore Massarro)
In his own quiet way, he was one of the most influential musicians of his day. Certainly no other side man was in as much demand.
Though of temperate habits, in 1933 he underwent a routine tonsillectomy and died of it!
His effect on Crosby was merely the tip of the iceberg. Lang's influence on a whole era of jazz and popular music was so pervasive that when he died, a significant piece of that era died with him.
Anyway, one day, I guess it was six or seven years ago, someone put out a CD of an obscure 30's crooner named Charlie Palloy.
Charlie Palloy
Vocals & Guitar
Crown Records
"2 hits for 2 bits"
Charlie Palloy, vocals & guitar

Apparently he made maybe two dozen sides that sold in dime stores for a quarter, when most records went for seventy-five cents or so, and still didn't sell too well 'cause who had a quarter to spare in 1933? Not too many if one of the songs on the CD, "Brother Can You Spare A Dime," is anything to go by.

Reading the liner notes, I found out that nobody seems to know who this Charlie Palloy really was other than that he seemed to be playing guitar as well as singing.

By crooner standards his voice wasn't exactly overwhelming me. His phrasing was full of "Crosbyisms" and had a lot of Russ Columbo in it too without being as good as either one of them.

But what about that guitar which was prominently on display on every side? Quite virile, particular and even hip, if I can be allowed

Brother can you spare a dime ♪ ///

CROWN RECORDS

that shopworn adjective. And eerily familiar too!

What was it reminding me of? The actual timbre of the voice wasn't that familiar.

And then on came the last song of the CD, a lilting, yet snappy version of "The Cop On The Beat, The Man In The Moon And Me",

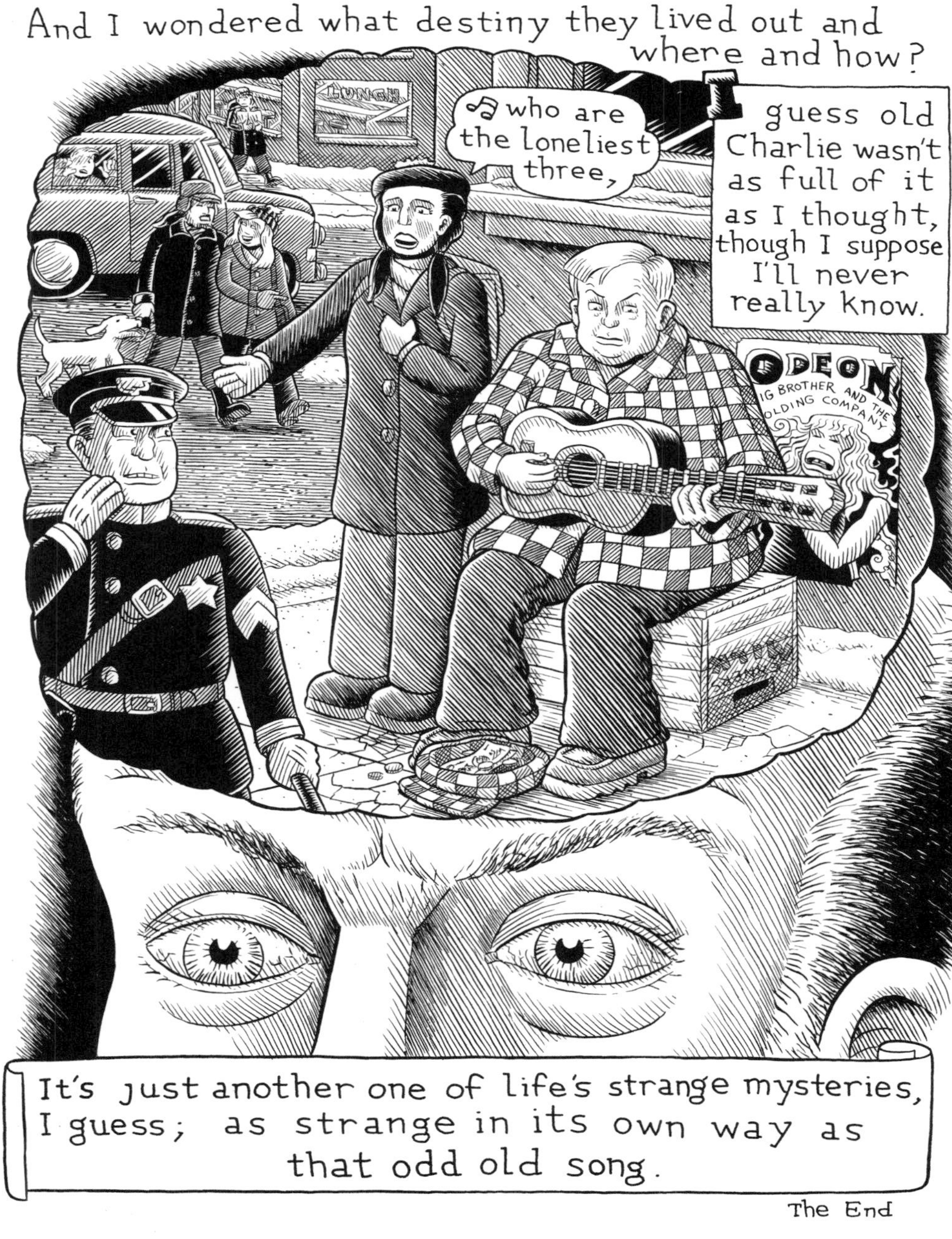
And I wondered what destiny they lived out and where and how?
LUNCH
♫ who are the loneliest three,
I guess old Charlie wasn't as full of it as I thought, though I suppose I'll never really know.
ODEON
IG BROTHER AND THE
OLDING COMPANY
It's just another one of life's strange mysteries, I guess; as strange in its own way as that odd old song.
The End

Further

ALIAS THE CAT
by Kim Deitch
Collecting Kim's most recent graphic novel extravaganza, the Eisner Award winning *Stuff of Dreams*, featuring Waldo the Cat!
(Pantheon, $23.00)

BEYOND THE PALE
by Kim Deitch
An oversized retrospective of Kim's 1970s and '80s work, this book includes classic stories from *Arcade*, *Snarf*, *The East Village Other* and more.
(Fantagraphics, $14.95)

THE COMICS JOURNAL #123
with Kim Deitch
Cover boy Kim speaks out in this far-ranging interview from the 1990s by Monte (*Blab*) Beauchamp. (Fantagraphics, $5.00)

A SHROUD FOR WALDO
by Kim Deitch
In this collected weekly serial from 1990, Waldo the Cat is embroiled in a strange tale of redemption, demons and Jesus Christ!
(Fantagraphics, $7.95)

SHADOWLAND
by Kim Deitch
Sexy Hollywood starlets, little gray aliens, flying pigs and performing elephants, sideshows, incest, murder, and eternal youth — it's all in here!
(Fantagraphics, $18.95)

Reading

BOULEVARD OF BROKEN DREAMS
by Kim and Simon Deitch
The epic saga of Golden Age animator Nate Mishkin and the not-quite-fictional Waldo the Cat — a story of treachery, corporate takeovers, infidelity, and madness. (Pantheon, $20.95)

MINESHAFT #18-20
with Simon Deitch
Each issue of this eclectic 'zine features art by Simon — plus, depending on the issue, Crumb, Stack, Griffith, Spiegelman, Spain, Fleener, et al. (Mineshaft, $6.95 each)

THE CAT ON A HOT THIN GROOVE
by Gene Deitch
A sumptuous hardcover collection of Gene's late-1940s *Record Changer* work, including the cartoon feature "The Cat" as well as almost all the covers. (Fantagraphics, $39.95)

TERR'BLE THOMPSON
by Gene Deitch
Gene's short-lived but charming strip about an odd little boy and his time-traveling adventures, co-starring many historic figures. (Fantagraphics, $18.95)

THE COMICS JOURNAL #293
with all 4 Deitches
This is the big one! Gary Groth grills Kim, Simon, Seth, and Gene Deitch, who have no choice but to spill all their beans! (Fantagraphics, $11.95)

Visit our website at www.fantagraphics.com, call us at 1-800-657-1100, or check your local comics or book store!

Biographical Notes

GENE DEITCH

Deitch is the name; I'm one of the Deitch boys. I was successfully born in 1924. Eighty-four years later I'm still working every day, trying to top that early success, but perhaps I peaked too soon. It was Chicago; the weather there was both too hot and too cold, and Hollywood seemed to be just right. So we moved there and that's where I grew up. I was left-handed and sensed that I was born to be a movie cartoon maker, and Hollywood was the place to be. Twenty years into my life I was already a published cartoonist. Even though it was only in a jazz fan mag, it was enough to get the attention of the UPA animation studio, and I was on my way to where I am now: more or less a has-been. The Oscar and the five nominations and most of the other gold-plated novelties are far in my past, but they got me into Wikipedia and Google, where you can look me up if you want, though neither mentions my greatest accomplishment, which was the fathering of three genius sons.

SIMON DEITCH

Since I was born in 1947, my life has had more ups and down than a biorhythm chart on horseback. I've been kickin' around the comic fandom racket in one form or another from the very beginning. I had my first artwork published in 1964 and worked the N.Y. convention scene from the get go. I slept on the floor of Gary Arlington's comic book store, the legendary San Francisco Comic Book Company, for the first year of the '70s and was Rory Hayes's roommate for the next two. Since then I've worked in animation, doing design work on the first two Nicktoons. I now continue to stay visible on the fanzine circuit. After three unsuccessful marriages I now make my home with a roommate and a diabetic cat.

SETH KALLEN DEITCH

I was born, so I am told, on a December morning in 1956, the youngest and least promising of three sons. Little did my parents suspect that I would grow up to be the first man to walk on the Moon! Of course, that lack of suspicion proved to be true. Had it only been true of those had by many guidance counselors and school psychologists that I was unlikely to rise to any particular distinction. As a youth, I ventured out into the wide world, hitchhiking its highways blissfully unaware of its not-so-well-hidden dangers. In short, I was an idiot. It remains unclear if that condition has altered to this day. I told stories then, I tell stories now, the only difference is that people call me "author" now rather than "liar." In this time, I have been held in the thrall of several muses, having made a mark in the arts of painting, collage and music, but the creation of stories has now held my attention well into its second decade. Wish me luck.

KIM DEITCH

I was born in Los Angeles in 1944. The atmosphere in the family was quite creative, sometimes volatile but never boring. I started drawing comics for publication in 1967, being influenced in that direction by both my Father and my brother Simon. My youngest brother Seth was a relative latecomer and kind of a sleeper too. But when he finally got his own head of steam up he quite blew me away. Put it all together and you begin to see why I had to get this book going and see it through. It was a rocky road at times but I think it was worth it. And I sincerely hope that you, the readers of this book, will think so too.